Angry Housewives

The Musical Comedy

Book by
A.M. Collins

Music and Lyrics by
Chad Henry

A SAMUEL FRENCH ACTING EDITION

SAMUEL FRENCH

FOUNDED 1830

New York Hollywood London Toronto

SAMUELFRENCH.COM

CAST

BEV is a widow, late 30's, early 40's. She has a son, Tim, and financial problems; is not used to coping for herself. Alto/guitar player.

CAROL is a high school teacher, early 30's. She is Tim's music and home room teacher. She is plump, divorced, and very self-sufficient. Mezzo/keyboard player.

JETTA is married to a lawyer, Larry, late 20's, early 30's. She has no self-confidence; went to college with Wendi. She has a baby, Annette. Soprano/accordion player.

WENDI is a drawbridge-tender, late 20's, early 30's. She has been dating Wallace for some time; went to college with Jetta. Very self-confident and energetic. Mezzo/drummer.

TIM is a high-school senior, 17 or 18. He is in Carol's home room and music classes. Tenor/lead guitar player.

WALLACE, mid-30's. Has been dating Wendi for some time; recently won $1,000,000 in a salmon derby. He is an attractive man, but a little insensitive. Went to college with Lewd Fingers. Tenor/tap-dancer.

LEWD FINGERS, is the owner/operator of a punk club by the same name, mid-30's. Went to college with Wallace. Baritone/tap-dancer.

LARRY, mid-30's, Jetta's husband. He is an up & coming lawyer, likes everything in it's place & Jetta's place is home. A bit anal-redentive he's confident & happy when things go according to his plan. High-Baritone-tenor.

Song:
LOVE O METER
SATURDAY NIGHT

SCENE 3 — Bon Poisson — Friday

Song:
NOBODY LOVES ME

SCENE 4 — Lewd Fingers on Friday night

Songs:
STALLING FOR TIME
MAN FROM GLAD
FINALE

Page 7

ANGRY HOUSEWIVES was presented by M Square Entertainment, Inc., Mitchell Maxwell, Alan J. Schuster, Marvin R. Meit, and Alice Field at the Minetta Lane Theatre, New York City, September 7, 1986, under the direction of Mitchell Maxwell. The Choreography was by Wayne Cilento, Scenery by David Jenkins, Lighting by Allen Lee Hughes, Costumes by Martha Hally, Sound by Otts Munderloh, Orchestrations by Dave Brown and Danny Troab, Additional Arrangements by Mark Hummel, Musical Direction by Jonny Bowden, Production Stage Manager, Clayton Phillips.

CAST

(*in order of appearance*)

BEV	Carolyn Casanave
TIM	Michael Manasseri
WENDY	Lorna Patterson
JETTA	Vicki Lewis
CAROL	Camille Saviola
LARRY	Nicholas Wyman
WALLACE	Michael Lembeck
LEWD FINGERS	Lee Wilcoff

ANGRY HOUSEWIVES was originally produced by Pioneer Square Theatre, Seattle, Wa., and subsequently produced by the Organic Theatre, Chicago, Il.

Originally produced at the Pioneer Square Theatre in Seattle, Washington, April 1983. Directed by Linda Hartzell with the following cast:

BEV	Barbara Benedetti
TIM	Jonathan Stewart
JETTA	Mary Van Arsdale
WENDY	Grechen Raumbaugh
WALLACE	Michael Smith
LEWD FINGERS	Randy Rogel

SET DESIGN: Edward J. Cunningham/J. C. Willis
COSTUMES: Alison Slaw Toris
SOUND: Nacho Bravo III
PROPS: Rich Nichols
LIGHTING: Steve Karns

Dedicated to
June and Mabel Henry
Mary Anne Collins and Anne Studeville

Angry Housewives

ACT ONE

Monday evening at BEV and TIM's.

SCENE 1

[MUSIC #1 HELL SCHOOL]

TIM starts to sing as the lights fade, "Hell School." Lights come up on him midway through. TIM, is a boy in his mid-teens dressed in messy and extremely ripped up clothing, with matted, badly dyed black hair and dark circles of make-up under his eyes.

TIM.
1,2,3,4
THEY MAKE YOU TAKE THESE CLASSES
THAT NO ONE EVER PASSES
AND ALL THE TEACHERS COME FROM THE
   TWILIGHT ZONE

NAH, NAH, NAH, NAH, NAH

THEY MAKE YOU TAKE HOT SHOWERS
AND READ AND WRITE FOR HOURS
FIRST THEY RIP YOUR FLESH
THEN THEY EAT YOUR BONES

(Lights come up, revealing his mother, who is setting up trays with make-up palats on them. She should only get around to setting up three. She holds a big pink book marked Betty Jean that she refers to.)

HELL SCHOOL
GET ME OUTTA HERE
HELL SCHOOL
YOU CAN'T WEAR LEATHER HERE
HELL SCHOOL
I THINK I'M TURNING QUEER
HELL SCHOOL
(It Ain't Pretty)

DON'T LET 'EM FIND YOU KISSIN'
OR ELSE YOU'LL END UP MISSIN'
THEY LOCK YOU DOWN IN THE BOILER ROOM
  WITH THE DIRT

NAH, NAH, NAH, NAH, NAH

THE PRINCIPAL'S INSANE
THE DEVIL ATE HIS BRAIN
EVERY TEACHER THERE IS A PER—ER—VERT

I DON'T WANNA GO
MAMA DON'T MAKE ME GO
MAMA PLEASE
MAMA PLEASE
MAMA, NO!

HELL SCHOOL
GET ME OUTTA HERE
HELL SCHOOL
YOU CAN'T WEAR LEATHER HERE
HELL SCHOOL
I THINK I'M TURNING QUEER
HELL SCHOOL
IT AIN'T PRETTY
HELL SCHOOL
IT AIN'T PRETTY
HELL SCHOOL
IT AIN'T PRETTY
HELL SCHOOL (*TIM makes strangling sounds on pitches*)

(*BEV throws down her book and yells up to TIM.*)

BEV. TIM! Shut the music off! It's too loud! (*She realizes it stopped.*) I'm trying to get ready for my make-up class.

TIM. That's cool, you ain't buggin me.

BEV. Thanks alot, I don't know why you kids have to play so loud! I can't . . .

BOTH. Hear myself think.

BEV. Very funny, Tim.

TIM. Can't I practice till your class gets here?

BEV. If you play quietly. I need to prepare for this.

TIM. It's me, me, me, with you all the time, isn't it?

BEV. I'm doing this for both of us. We could make alot of money here tonight.

TIM. Man, be real. This stuff is a bust.

BEV. That's not true, not if you sell alot of it.

TIM. How many are coming?

BEV. I invited 39. . . .

TIM. (*sarcastically*) Right, and they're all comin, huh?

BEV. Oh yes, I've been thinking positive about this all week.

TIM. (*Exasperated*) Oh mom, you always think positive and it never works. We're still broke.

BEV. I found out I've been doing it all wrong. (*She reads from her large pink notebook.*) See, it says here: Don't dwell on your problems, that just makes things worse. Form a mental picture of your ideal situation and color it with a pretty pink glow.

(*During the following song BEV feverishly picks up the house, folding laundry etc. and otherwise preparing for the Betty Jean make-up demonstration. By the end of the song the house is magically transformed. Sung:*)

[MUSIC #2 *THINK POSITIVE*]

BEV.
THINK POSITIVE
THINK PERKY, THINK PINK
THINK POSITIVE, THOUGH IT SOUNDS RINKY-DINK.
SAY YOU'RE SLOUCHED IN A SLUM
CAUSE THE UNIVERSE TREATS YOU LIKE SCUM.
DON'T SIT AROUND ASKING HOW COME
DRY THAT TEAR, GET YOUR BEHIND IN GEAR
AND THINK POSITIVE, STARTING RIGHT HERE.
(*spoken*)
MY LIFE IS GETTING BETTER AND BETTER
MY LIFE IS GETTING BETTER AND BETTER

TIM. I worry about you mom, maybe you should see a shrink. (*The phone rings.*)

BEV. (*grabs it*) Hello?

TIM. I mean thinking is one thing, doing is another.

BEV. Quiet, Tim. Sandi, hi! Oh—you can't make it? I understand. Hope it's not malignant. (*sung*)
THINK POSITIVE, YOU'LL NEVER FAIL.
THINK POSITIVE GET ON THE HAPPY TRAIL.
SAY YOUR FRIENDS ARE ALL FINKS

AND THERE'S PERMANENT STAINS IN YOUR SINK.
PAINT YOUR WORLD A PASSIONATE PINK
AND KAPOW! TELL YOUR TROUBLES CIAO!
JUST THINK POSITIVE, STARTING NOW.
(*Phone rings again. Spoken:*) Hello?

TIM. Mom, I'm just trying to help you out. What about that janitor job at Jack in the Box?

BEV. Tim, I mean it! Hush. Oh, hello Misty. You can't come? And Rhonda and Tawny and Cheryl can't come either? (*Aside*) Damn. Your grandmothers ALL died? Hello? Hello? (*She hangs up. Sung:*)
COLOR MY WORLD WONDERFUL
I'M HAVING A MARVELOUS TIME
THOUGH MY HUSBAND IS DEAD.
(*She fights back a breakdown, then recovers angrily.*)
AND HE DIDN'T LEAVE A GODDAMNED DIME!
(*spoken, cheerily*) No problem, we're fine. (*sung*)
COLOR MY WORLD GLAMOROUS
THOUGH I HAVEN'T FOUND A JOB SO FAR.
AND, OH YES, THEY'RE GONNA REPOSSESS THE CAR!
(*spoken*) Please God, not the car! (*sung*)
BUT WE STILL HAVE THIS CUTE LITTLE
SPLIT LEVEL RANCH
BY THE A&P AND THE DRIVE IN BRANCH
OF THE BANK WHERE I CAN'T PAY THE
MORTGAGE THAT'S DUE.
IT'S A NIGHTMARE COME TRUE.
IT'S DIEN BIEN PHU!
IT'S AN AVALANCHE
(*spoken*) I'm Happy! I'm confused (*to TIM*) Turn it down I can't think (*to TIM*) Turn it down! (*sung*)
AND MY CUTE LITTLE SON IS A PUNK AND A TWINK
I'M LONELY, I'M SCARED
SCARED, HELL, I'M HYSTERICAL
I NEED A MIRACLE.
(*She sinks to her knees.*)
I NEED A DRINK!
(*She reaches for the bottle, stops herself.*)
NO! NO!
(*almost takes one*)
WELL?
(*overcomes the urge*)
NO!!!!

THINK POSITIVE, THINK PERKY THINK PINK
THINK POSITIVE
THINK CADILLACS, DIAMONDS AND MINKS.
I'M SECURE, I'M SUCCESSFUL, I'M PRETTY!!
LIFE'S EXCITING
(*spoken*) Life is shitty (*sternly*) Don't say that. (*sung*)
THINK POSITIVE
IT'LL TURN YOUR WORLD AROUND!

(*End of song — she's very cheered.*)

TIM. Well don't positive think too much and implode your brain.

(*He exits back to his room as WENDI and JETTA enter.*)

WENDI. Sorry we're late. (*She looks around.*) Where is everybody?
BEV. This is it so far.
JETTA. How many did you invite?
BEV. Thirty-nine.
JETTA. (*aghast*) Thirty-NINE?
WENDI. I can't believe Carol didn't show.

(*From off*)

CAROL. I'm here! (*She enters eating.*) I came through the back and accidently opened the fridge. What are these? (*indicating what she's eating*) Spaghetti sandwiches? (*The others gag.*)
BEV. Those are for later, Carol. Let's get started, okay?
CAROL. They're pretty good, even if the spaghetti IS al dente.
BEV. (*seating the others*) Welcome to the wonderful world of Betty Jean . . . (*TIM starts up again.*)
TIM. (*off*)
HELL SCHOOL LORD GET ME OUTTA HERE!!!
BEV. Tim!!!!!! Shut it off!! Tim!!!
TIM. (*off*) What?
BEV. My class is here! You'll have to stop now.
TIM. (*off*) Yeah, yeah — let me know when you've made your million.
CAROL. I didn't know Tim wrote music.
JETTA. You're his music teacher.
BEV. Yes, he said you inspired that song. Okay — here we go.

(*BEV opens a large pink book and reads.*) Welcome to the wonderful, magical world of Betty Jean Cosmetics. We will begin by singing the Betty Jean Anthem. (*On each of the trays are song sheets. The other women grab a song sheet as BEV switches on a portable tape recorder, that they sing along with.*)

[MUSIC #3: *BETTY JEAN*]

ALL.
BETTY JEAN, BETTY JEAN, BETTY JEAN,
OUR PRODUCTS WILL BRING THE GLOW OF
    YOUTH TO YOU
LIKE ROSES IN THE MORNING DEW
IS YOUR COMPLEXION DRY?
GIVE BETTY JEAN A TRY.
THAT'S SKIN CARE PRODUCTS BY.
BETTY JEAN, BETTY JEAN, BETTY JEAN, BETTY JEAN
BETTY JEAN!!!!

BEV. Now I will read to you the history of Betty Jean Cosmetics while you apply the cucumber cleansing cream. (*She pauses nervously.*) I'm a little nervous.

WENDI. You're doing great, go on.

BEV. Oh and remember to use your sterile plastic applicators. (*The women apply the cream as they speak.*) Betty Jean was discovered by a garage mechanic in Teaneck, New Jersey who found that crankcase oil kept his skin as young and smooth as the underbelly of a dolphin. (*During this speech she opens the pink notebook to pictures of Betty Jean, the garage mechanic and finally a dolphin. On crankcase oil the women stop applying the cream, looking slightly aghast. They each grab a jar to read the ingredients.*)

CAROL. Wait, wait—can't we eat a little something now?

BEV. It says to wait till *after* class.

CAROL. Please?! I have to eat a little something every half hour or I go beserk and have to eat alot.

BEV. (*exasperated*) Oh, alright! But we have over 500 products to get through and we haven't even made it to the first one yet. (*BEV exits to kitchen.*)

CAROL. What can I say? Divorce has done wonders for my appetite.

WENDI. How long has it been since your divorce?

CAROL. Let's see. . . . I've gained 40 pounds—so it's 2 months.

BEV. (*entering with sandwiches*) We're getting off the track here, beauty now—girl talk later. (*CAROL grabs a handful of spaghetti sandwiches. The others look at them in disgust. BEV notices this and is hurt.*) Well, I'm sorry, it's all I could afford. (*WENDI and JETTA each grab one and try to eat it.*)

JETTA. Carol, do you miss Raoul?

CAROL. I miss the company, I was married to the guy since I was 22.

JETTA. That's almost how old I was, except I was 25.

BEV. (*angrily*) Would anyone mind too much if we continued?

JETTA. Sorry.

WENDI. Go on.

CAROL. We're listening.

(*TIM enters.*)

TIM. Hey, mom, how's the scam goin? Gettin any money outta them?

BEV. Ha ha ha ha, you're so cute! (*hisses at him*) What do you want?

TIM. Five bucks.

BEV. Why?

TIM. They're having this contest at Lewd Fingers Saturday. See, the best band wins $2,000. My band is gonna enter. (*shows her a flyer*)

JETTA. Lewd Fingers?

BEV. It's an underage Disco.

TIM. Punk club, mom!

BEV. Punk club. Tim, we don't have it.

TIM. (*loudly*) What about the fifty Grandma sent me for my birthday?

BEV. (*so the others won't hear*) Shh! I told you we need that for bills.

TIM. (*so the others will hear*) It's my money! I should at least get five of it!

BEV. Shhhh! (*then, angrily*) Oh, alright, here you go.

TIM. Thanks Queen of all Moms.

BEV. (*She can't help but love him.*) Oh, you. (*She touches his hair affectionately and they both recoil.*)

TIM. Mom, it took me three hours and five cans of mousse to get my hair right. Now I have to do it all over. (*He exits slamming the door. BEV wipes her hand but the tissue sticks.*)

BEV. (*to herself*)

My life is getting better and better.
My life is getting better and better.
Carol, what are you doing?

CAROL. This cucumber crankcase stuff is delicious on these sandwiches.

BEV. (*throwing the book down*) Hey! Alright! I have just one little question. Are any of you going to buy any of this crap or am I just wasting my breath?

CAROL. I'd like to, but since the teachers strike, I'm flat broke.

WENDI. I just came to be supportive.

JETTA. I might have some money.

WENDI. No you don't. You borrowed my last five for your kid's toothcutting liquid.

JETTA. I might have some surprise money. (*She looks and doesn't.*) Surprise.

BEV. Fine, fine. It's perfectly, perfectly . . . terrible. (*She begins to cry.*) It's been so hard since Roger died. The savings are all gone. I can't find a job. If I just hadn't shown him the bills before dinner. It was the electric bill that did it.

CAROL. Don't blame yourself.

JETTA. No, don't. It could have been anything you did that killed him.

WENDI. Jetta! Shhh!

JETTA. Sorry!

WENDI. This stuff never makes any money—there's too many people selling it. Let's think! Did you do anything before you met Roger?

BEV. Sold Avon. (*They look depressed.*) Played Guitar in the church choir. (*They look more depressed.*) Oh, it's hopeless.

WENDI. (*looking at flyer*) Ladies, I think I have an idea.

BEV. You do?

WENDI. Yep, and if it works, we could have five-hundred dollars each by Saturday.

BEV. That would hold me for awhile.

CAROL. What is it?

WENDI. Can you come to the bridge tomorrow? I want to think this through before I tell you. (*Doorbell rings.*)

BEV. Hey! Maybe someone showed up to buy this junk after all.

(*LARRY enters with a briefcase handcuffed to him.*)

LARRY. Jetta, chop chop, let's go. I don't want to miss my quiet time. By the time we drop Wendi off, I'll have missed 3 and 3 quarter minutes of it.

JETTA. Oh, of course honey. I'll get my coat.

LARRY. So, how did your little make-up class go?

BEV. Just fine, Larry.

WENDI. How's your little court case going?

LARRY. Little? It's my biggest case yet, Pardon Moi! But I'm really not at liberty to talk about it.

BEV. (*relieved*) Oh, well.

LARRY. But you gals just have to know everything, don't you? Heh Heh You heard about the high school that kicked the girl off the cheerleading squad for having hairy legs?

BEV. You're representing the girl? Good for you! That's a landmark case!

LARRY. That hairy little hippie? No! The school board! Ready Jetta?

JETTA. Yes, dear. Where's Annette?

LARRY. In the car with my mommy, er mother.

JETTA. Your Mother?!?!?!?!?!

LARRY. Well there wasn't anything prepared to eat so I had her cab over to fix me something to eat.

JETTA. Oh no! Wendi, let's go!

WENDI. Okay, so I'll see you guys at the bridge tomorrow and I'll tell you the idea then.

LARRY. Oh-oh. Another one of Wendi's weird ideas?

JETTA. It's just an idea for Bev to make money. Don't worry.

LARRY. Just keep my poor Jetta out of it. She's got enough to do with me and baby Annette.

CAROL. You can say that again. (*They exit. LARRY, JETTA and WENDI exit. TIM cranks up his music and resumes screaming/feedback.*)

BEV. Tim!

TIM. Now what?!

BEV. You're going to have to turn it down or the neighbor is going to complain.

TIM. Tell the neighbor to piss off.

BEV. Sweetie, either keep it down or don't play it at all. (*TIM slams the door*)

BEV. If this idea doesn't pan out I could always join the Peace Corps. They pay 175 a week. But what would I do with Tim?

CAROL. I don't know. Put him in a kennel?

BEV. Carol! Please, he's my son. (*TIM cranks up his music and howls. CAROL and BEV look at each other in surprise.*)

BLACKOUT

SCENE 2

Tuesday Afternoon
The Bridge

(*WENDI is at work at the drawbridge. There are two windows—one to see the boats and one to see bridge traffic. There is a control panel with buttons, levers and a small screen.* WENDI is sitting and reading a punk magazine. In the distance you can hear boat horns and people yelling. She is listening to a hard core punk song. WALLACE enters. He is a rather handsome man dressed in typical boating clothes except he wears a funny-looking hat with fishing lures and other fishing stuff on it.*)

WALLACE. Wendi! What the Beegeebees are ya doin?

WENDI. Ah . . . Oh! Oh . . . (*She turns off the tape recorder.*) I didn't even hear them! (*She checks the boat traffic, stops the vehicular traffic and raises the bridge.*)

WALLACE. You got to pay attention to your job!

WENDI. I know that. I just didn't hear 'em, that's all.

WALLACE. Good golly, no wonder. The music was playing so loud.

WENDI. (*coy*) Hello, Wally. Did you come up to see me? Or to yell at me?

WALLACE. I came up here so that some boater wouldn't call the Port Authority to find out why the hell the bridge didn't go up.

WENDI. Is that all?

WALLACE. Yeah.

WENDI. Don't I get a kiss? (*WALLACE gives her a perfunctory peck.*)

WALLACE. Wait 'till you see the work I did on the boat today! It

---

There is a large log book and a P.A. microphone.

looks top notch, I'm tellin' ya. I painted the name on the stern, DERBY KING. Big letters.

WENDI. All you ever talk about is the boat and that silly derby.

WALLACE. Winning the salmon derby has made me a millionaire.

WENDI. Oh, I know. But sometimes I think you love them more than you love me.

WALLACE. No way José. I love you the same.

WENDI. Wallace!

WALLACE. I mean, I love you first, then the fish, and then the boat. If I hadn't won that salmon derby, I'd still be selling rudders. Now we can do like we always planned to — take a trip.

WENDI. Oh, it's going to be so romantic, sailing to Hawaii. (*She hums Aloha-O.*)

WALLACE. I can just see us — sailin' into the harbor. Me at the helm, you by my side. The waves kinda lappin' up against the side of the boat, palm trees swayin' in the breeze, lovers walking hand-in-hand along the shore, and all of them stopping to admire the DERBY KING.

WENDI. Wallace!

WALLACE. What'd I say? Jeez, you're touchy today.

WENDI. I am not touchy. You're insensitive.

WALLACE. (*He sees magazine & reads title.*) Bleeding Ears?? What kind of comic book is this?

WENDI. (*Hiding it*) Oh, nothing. Nothing at all.

WALLACE. What are you up to?

WENDI. Up to? Ha, ha. Now, Wally, you know me better than that.

WALLACE. Is that why you're listening to that music? You're not taking that crap on the trip, are ya?

WENDI. No. It's just a dumb idea I had, that's all.

WALLACE. Well, what is it? You're *not* getting another job! We got a lot of work to do on the boat. We leave in a month.

WENDI. I don't want to tell you, because I know you'll laugh.

WALLACE. I won't laugh.

WENDI. Yes you will.

WALLACE. No I won't.

WENDI. Really?

WALLACE. Really.

WENDI. We're gonna start a punk rock group.

WALLACE. (*a beat*) No, really, what is it?

WENDI. I'm serious Wallace. Look at this. We're going to start a band and we're gonna win this $2,000. See, best punk rock group.

WALLACE. Boy Howdy, Wendi, you crack me up! (*He laughs hysterically.*)

WENDI. You promised not to laugh.

WALLACE. That was before you told me. Where is this place?

WENDI. Lewd Fingers, see?

WALLACE. Lewd Fingers?

WENDI. Listen, we only have to play one song.

WALLACE. We? Who are you doin' this with?

WENDI. Bev, Carol and Jetta.

WALLACE. (*laughs*) Why don't you just go in and rob the place? It'd be a hell of a lot easier.

WENDI. I know we can do this—come on.

WALLACE. Jeepers, please let me pay for the trip.

WENDI. No, no. It's more than just the money. It's the excitement, the risk.

WALLACE. Seriously, Wendi, I've heard about these places. They bite the heads off of bats and chickens!

WENDI. They do not! *Those* are *geeks.* I didn't say we were playing in a *geek* club.

JETTA. (*from offstage*) Wendi!

WENDI. (*to WALLACE*) Don't say anything, I haven't told them yet.

(*JETTA appears at the door. She is winded.*)

JETTA. Gosh, Wendi—do you climb up and down those stairs every day? They make me dizzy.

WENDI. I'm sorry.

JETTA. (*to WALLACE*) Oh, hi! How are you? Gosh, I haven't seen you since you won that fishing contest.

WALLACE. It wasn't a contest, it was a fishing *derby!* Hey, you want to see a picture?

JETTA. Okay.

WALLACE. There's me on the left, and there's the fish on the right.

JETTA. That's the winning fish?

WALLACE. Uh huh.

JETTA. Why is it so small?

WALLACE. It's a *tag* fish, not a *weight* fish. It doesn't matter how much it weighs. You see, they put a little tag . . .

WENDI. Wally, didn't you say you were leaving?

WALLACE. Oh, right. Bye, Jetta.

JETTA. Bye bye.

WENDI. Hey, don't I get a kiss before you go?

(*They kiss, for a long time. CAROL and BEV enter. They are out of breath.*)

CAROL. Do you climb up that ladder every day? I think I'm hyperventilating.

JETTA. (*Indicating WENDI and WALLY*) Shhh.

CAROL. That happened to me once.

WENDI. Hi guys.

WALLACE. (*embarrassed*) Hi guys. You shouldn't have to see that, sorry.

WENDI. Oh c'mon, they don't mind, do you?

CAROL. Oh no, I love living vicariously.

WALLACE. Well you won't be gettin' anymore kisses after you start biting off bat heads. (*WALLACE exits. The women look at each other, confused.*)

BEV. What's *that* mean?

WENDI. Oh, you know sailor's twisted sense of humor.

CAROL. Alright, Wendi — what's this idea? I put off my afternoon snack.

JETTA. I put off delinting Larry's socks.

WENDI. Okay, sit down. Now, before I say anything, I just want to say that I know I've had some pretty bad ideas before but *this* one *is* really good.

BEV. Will you get to the point? I have a job interview at Jack in the Box.

WENDI. Forget the job interview — THIS is the point. (*She plays the tape.*)

CAROL. We're going to get jobs in riot control?

WENDI. NO! We're going to start our own punk band. (*BEV, CAROL and JETTA look at each other in surprise and then realize she must be kidding.*)

BEV. Don't scare me like that.

CAROL. No, really — c'mon.

WENDI. I'm serious! (*BEV and CAROL get up to leave.*)

BEV. Looks like it's Jack in the Box for me.

CAROL. You made us come all the way up here for THIS? I should kill you!

JETTA. Want one of my stress tabs?

WENDI. (*Stopping them*) Wait, we could have five hundred dollars each by Saturday!!!

CAROL. (*They stop.*) I could lose my job over something like this.

BEV. I can't compete against my own son.

WENDI. To save your house and car you could.

CAROL. We're too old.

WENDI. No we're not. See all the other bands look and sound alike. We'll be *different.*

BEV. You got that right. We'll be so different they'll kill us.

WENDI. Not if we're great!

JETTA. Kill us? Great! I can just see Larry's face.

WENDI. He doesn't have to know. Besides we only have to have one song. Bev — you play guitar!

BEV. Jesus Loves Me, and Kumbayah.

WENDI. And Carol — you play piano.

CAROL. Rumanian Folk ballads.

WENDI. And Jetta, what do you play?

JETTA. I used to play accordian, but that didn't really fit into Larry's corporate image. Besides, he'd be so upset if I came home with safety pins sticking out of me.

WENDI. This could be *fun*!

BEV. This could be weird!

WENDI. Exciting!

CAROL. Weird!

JETTA. Very, very weird.

WENDI. What a bunch of wienies. I don't know why I hang around with you. You don't know what fun is.

[MUSIC #4: *IT'S GONNA BE FUN*]

LISTEN TO YOU, JUST LISTEN TO YOU, YOU'RE
    DRIVING ME NUTS
LISTEN TO YOU, JUST LISTEN TO ALL YOUR IFS
    & ANDS & BUTS
YOU'VE NO SENSE OF ADVENTURE, YOU'RE LIKE
    A BUNCH OF NUNS
DAMMIT, DONCHA KNOW THAT LIFE IS SUPPOSED
    TO BE FUN

IF YOU'RE INTO MOPPING AND GOING OUT
    SHOPPING FOR UNDERWEAR AND SHOES
IF YOU'RE INTO BAKING AND PILLS YOU ARE

TAKING FOR YOUR PREMENSTRUAL BLUES
THAT'S OKAY WITH ME, IT'S PERFECTLY OKAY
   WITH ME.
BUT YOU'RE STARTING TO RUST SO PARDON MY
   DUST HEY I GOTTA RUN
LIFE IS SUPPOSED TO BE FUN

NO! YOU'RE BUYING A HONDA AND SWEATING
   WITH FONDA AND TAKING TOO MUCH ASPIRIN
YOU TALK ABOUT FOOTBALL AND WHO'S DOING
   WHAT-ALL TO WHO ON ALL MY CHILDREN
THAT'S OKAY WITH ME IF THAT'S THE WAY YOU
   WANNA BE
BUT YOU'RE REALLY A BORE THERE'S GOT TO
   BE MORE, HEY I GOTTA RUN
LIFE IS SUPPOSED TO BE FUN

CLIMB OUTTA YOUR RUTS (OH WENDY) STOP
   ACTING YOUR AGES (NO WENDY)
GET OFFA YOUR BUTTS, SET YOURSELF FREE
(OH HERE WE GO AGAIN)
CLIMB OUTTA YOUR RUTS (WE WISH WE WOULD)
BUST OUTTA YOUR CAGES (WE WISH WE COULD)
GET OFFA YOUR BUTTS, AND LISTEN TO ME IT'S
   GOING TO BE
OUTRAGEOUS (OUTRAGEOUS)

CAROL. You promise this'll work, and it won't be a different story later?

WENDI. Promise.

BEV. As long as Tim doesn't know.

WENDI. We'll be in disguise.

JETTA. You guys, this sounds like fun!

WENDI. Now you're talking!!

ALL.

TO HELL WITH THE HOUSEWORK
(WENDY) IT'S ALL MICKEY MOUSE WORK
OUR LUCKY STAR IS RISING
IT'S GONNA BE CHAMPAGNE
(WENDY) AND LIFE IN THE FAST LANE
WHEN WE START HARMONIZING

WENDY.	WOMEN.
OH BABY	BABY

OH BABY	BABY
I REALLY LOVE YOU	I REALLY LOVE YOU
I WANT YOU	BABY
I NEED YOU	BABY
OH BABY	YOU DRIVE ME CRAZY
YOU GOT TO	YEAH
HOLD ME	YEAH
SQUEEZE ME	YEAH

ALL.
NEVER LEAVE ME BABY

IT'S GONNA BE GREAT, I HARDLY CAN WAIT TO
  GRAB THE BALL AND RUN YEAH IT'S GONNA BE

WENDY.	WOMEN.
A RAMPAGE	FUN
A RIOT	FUN
A PARTY	FUN

ALL.
A PARTY YEAH
IT'S GONNA BE
YEAH IT'S GONNA BE FUN
        FUN OH YEAH, FUN OH YEAH
        IT'S GONNA BE FUN YEAH

(*Larry enters and we hear a baby crying.*)

LARRY. (*to the baby*) Shh, shh, Annette, don't cry—look, daddy's making a funny face! See? (*Baby cries louder.*) Will you stop being such a baby? You don't see *daddy* crying because mommy is 15 minutes late. (*He cries. He dials the phone.*) Hello, this is Mr. Prince. Mr. Larry Prince, Junior Partner. Are there any messages from my wife? You haven't been taking them? Who is this? Debbi? Well, Debbi, this is a disgrace. I could have your ass going out the door so fast you'd think it had grown propellers. OOOhhh. . . . I'm scared . . . you're going to tell your big bad daddy on poor Wawwy? . . . oh boo hoo hoo. . . . . . . Who? *That's* your daddy? Oh well, uh, Debbi, I caught you. You fell for the old propeller joke! Ha ha ha! No, no, no don't bother your pretty head with messages, I'll call back. Okay. Sure. Bye bye. Bye bye.

(*He stabs himself with phone, then re-dials. Phone rings. Lights up on TIM as he answers.*)

TIM. Hello?

LARRY. Hello, this is Mr. Prince.

TIM. Who?

LARRY. Mr. Larry Prince, Junior Partner, and Jetta's husband. Is she there?

TIM. Nah, they went out to get a beer or something.

LARRY. Beer? Jetta and I hate beer.

TIM. I don't know man, I think that's where they went. My mom never tells me anything, you know — women. . . .

LARRY. I know a few women, I couldn't possibly know all women.

TIM. Look, you wanna leave a message or what? I'm busy.

LARRY. When they get back, could you tell Jetta that she's now seventeen minutes late and that her husband and child are sitting at home waiting for their dinner, and. . . .

TIM. Please tell Jetta . . . is that with a J or a G?

LARRY. Forget it.

TIM. Okay. (*Baby cries louder*)

LARRY. Hey do you know how to stop a baby from crying?

TIM. Sure. Hit it.

BLACKOUT

[MUSIC #4A: *FUN PLAYOFF*]

SCENE 3

*Late Wednesday afternoon. Lights come up revealing a rehearsal. BEV is playing accoustic guitar, JETTA the accordian, CAROL a small handheld autoharp and WENDY a bass drum. They are playing an off-key and out-of-sync African hymn, such as "Kumbaya"**

WENDI. Ladies, this is supposed to be rock and roll. Play it faster.

(*They sing off-key and out of sync again, only faster.*)

CAROL. Wait! Stop! (*They stop.*) We aren't *playing* together.

---

*Note: permission to produce ANGRY HOUSEWIVES does *not* include rights to use any material not the property of the Authors. For such permission, contact A.S.C.A.P. or B.M.I., New York City.

WENDI. Give us the note again, Carol. And Jetta, you have to at *least* play the tune.

JETTA. But I don't remember how to play this thing. And it's so heavy, it's squishing my boobs.

BEV. Are you holding it right?

JETTA. I don't know. I haven't played this since I was ten. And I didn't have boobs then.

WENDI. One more time. I know we can do this. (*She counts off on Bass drum.*)

(*They all sing again, just as terrible as before.*)

CAROL. That's it! That's it! STOP!!!!! This is killing my sinuses.

WENDI. Don't give up, we've only been at this for . . . (*They all check their watches.*)

ALL. Two and a half hours. (*They all sit down defeated.*)

BEV. It just doesn't work with us all banging away at the same time. Besides, the only rock song I ever learned was "House of The Rising Sun."

WENDI. Don't give up. Let's play the tape again. (*She plays the tape from the last scene, they all listen jiggling to the beat.*) I've got it!!! We've got to play it meaner!

CAROL. It would be hard to play a mean Kumbaya.

WENDI. Let's start with the name. See, all punk bands have mean names, like: Swollen Monkey's, Pig Vomit, Butthole Surfers. . . .

CAROL. How about The Jello Thighs?

WENDI. Not mean enough. How about. . . . (*She gets a burst of inspiration.*) I know! . . . Angry Housewives?! (*The others are unimpressed.*)

JETTA. Does that mean we have to be angry all the time?

WENDI. Not really. More seething and tough and cool.

BEV. Seething. Angry. Angry Housewives. (*Acting it out:*) "I'm a housewife and I'm angry, so you pick your damn clothes up!!!"

WENDI. Great! But one thing I've noticed about these kids is that nothing seems to phase them, like, Clint Eastwood when he guns down 11 people with one bullet. (*indicating face*) Nothing. Try that.

BEV. (*ala Clint*) "So, you'd rather watch TV than do your homework, eh punk? Well go ahead, *make my day.*" (*She crushes a beer can in one hand, they all cheer.*)

JETTA. Can I try? My turn!

WENDI. Sure, go ahead.

JETTA. Seething, right?

WENDI. Yeah.

JETTA. "Alright you little baby, take off those diapers! Take 'em off. (*She mimes a gun.*) Slow. Now drop 'em. Bang!"

WENDI. Very good, Jetta! Very seething. But most punks aren't really killers.

CAROL. But you *said* Clint Eastwood.

WENDI. His attitude.

CAROL. Can I try? Pretend I'm wearing sunglasses & smoking a cigarette "I'm only gonna say this once. Eat your fucking cornflakes." (*WENDI and BEV collapse in laughter.*)

WENDI. Perfect! Hey, what a great idea for a song! Eat Your Fucking Cornflakes." (*WENDI begins to chant it, BEV and CAROL join in.*)

WENDI, CAROL & BEV. Eat your fucking cornflakes, Eat your fucking cornflakes!! Eat your fucking cornflakes!!!!

JETTA. Wait, wait, wait! That's *dirty! I* can't say that!

WENDI. We're going to sing it, not say it.

JETTA. But I just wouldn't feel right about saying it.

BEV. How about "Frigging?"

JETTA. It's pretty close to the "F" word.

WENDI. Oh, try it.

JETTA. (*It's very painful.*) F-F-F-F-F-Frigging. Eat-your-frigging-cornflakes. (*Everyone cheers.*)

WENDI. There you go!

JETTA. (*in distress*) Larry's gonna be real mad when he finds out about this.

WENDI. He's not going to know. Besides, we'll be in disguise.

CAROL. I hope so, cause I'd hate to be up there as me. I feel so fat & old.

WENDI. (*She's said this before.*) You *aren't* fat & old!

CAROL. Heavy & aging?

JETTA. You aren't that fat & old. (*Everyone glares at her.*) Well, you aren't!

CAROL. You've never been to the beach with me. Mass Hysteria. Last time I went . . . I caught a harpoon.

WENDI. Carol, you're an attractive woman.

BEV. Yes, you are.

JETTA. You have a beautiful FACE!

CAROL. (*insulted*) Thanks alot. But I know I'm no Miss America.

BEV. None of us are. But you know it says in my positive thinking book that to be pretty you have to think pretty.

CAROL. I've tried that stuff. It never works for me.

[MUSIC #5: *GENERIC WOMEN*]

WHEN I'M WALKING DOWN THE STREET
ALL THE MEN I'D LIKE TO MEET
ARE SMILING AT THE GIRL
IT'S NOT THE BOOK, IT'S THE COVER
THEY LOOK FOR IN A LOVER
IF THEY TOOK THE TIME
THEY WOULD FIND ME
CAUSE I'M A MAJOR BRAND

WENDI, BEV & JETTA.	CAROL.
IN A PLAIN WRAPPER	I'M A MAJOR BRAND
IN A PLAIN WRAPPER	I'M A MAJOR

ALL.
BRAND, IN A PLAIN WRAPPER
GENERIC WOMAN

CAROL.	OTHERS.
SOMETIMES IT CAUSES ME PAIN	OOOH, OOOH, OOOH,
THAT MY PACKAGE IS SO PLAIN	THAT HER PACKAGE IS PLAIN
AND THAT MOST OF MY CHARMS ARE ALL	OOOH, OOOH, OOOH,

ALL.
HIDDEN

CAROL.	OTHERS.
BUT BEAUTY'S ONLY SKIN DEEP	OOOH, OOOH, OOOH,
SO LISTEN TO ME YOU CREEP	LISTEN TO ME YOU CREEP
I'M THE TOP OF THE LINE I AIN'T	OOOH, OOOH, OOOH,

ALL.
KIDDIN

CAROL.	OTHERS.
NO NO	NO NO
I'M A MAJOR BRAND	BUT IN A PLAIN WRAPPER

I'M A MAJOR BRAND   BUT IN A PLAIN WRAPPER
I'M A MAJOR
   ALL.
BRAND
GENERIC WOMAN
HEY MAN
   CAROL.   OTHERS.
IF YOU'RE LOOKING FOR   HEY MAN, COME ON,
  REAL KISSING   COME ON
TRY A REAL WOMAN   I'M ONLY HUMAN
TONIGHT   HEY MAN
HEY MAN

                  WANNA KNOW WHAT

IF YOU WANNA KNOW
WHAT   YOUR
YOU'RE MISSIN   MISSIN

IT'S WRITTEN ALL OVER ME IN BLACK AND WHITE
  (AHHH)

   OTHERS.   CAROL.
GENERIC WOMAN   GENERIC WOMAN
GENERIC WOMAN   GENERIC WOMAN
GENERIC WOMAN   GENERIC WOMAN
GENERIC   WOMAN (BEV)
            WOMAN (JETTA.)
            WOMAN (WENDY.)
            WOMAN (CAROL.)
   CAROL.   OTHERS.
WHEN I'M WALKING   WALKIN DOWN THE
  DOWN THE STREET   STREET
ALL THE MEN I'D LIKE   CRUISIN, CRUISIN
  TO MEET
ARE SMILING AT THE   WATCH YOURSELF
  GIRL
BEHIND ME   BEHIND ME
IT'S NOT THE BOOK IT'S   IT'S NOT THE BOOK IT'S
  THE COVER   THE COVER
THAT THEY LOOK FOR   THAT THEY LOOK FOR
  IN A LOVER   IN A LOVER
IF THEY ONLY TOOK   DON'T WASTE MY TIME
  THE TIME

THEY WOULD FIND ME
CAUSE I'M A MAJOR
  BRAND

            DOO DOO DOO

I'M A MAJOR BRAND

            DOO DOO DOO

I'M A MAJOR BRAND

            DOO DOO DOO

I'M A WOMAN
  ALL. WOMAN, WOMAN, WOMAN, WOMAN, WOMAN, WOMAN, WOMAN, WOMAN, WOMAN, WOMAN, WOMAN, WOMAN, WOMAN, WOMAN, WOMAN, WOMAN, WOMAN, WOMAN

GENERIC WOMAN (3 RIMSHOTS)
  CAROL. WOMAN WOMAN WOMAN
WOMAN
  WENDI. Now, let's get back to work.
  CAROL. Let's eighty-six the accordian.
  JETTA. Now I don't have an instrument to play, I don't have a disguise, and I have to sing a dirty song. That doesn't sound like much fun to *me*.
  WENDI. You get to look at all the cute boys *and* you can be the lead singer! Hey does anyone know "House of the Rising Sun?"
  CAROL. Do I? I ate my first Dorito to that song. Bev, A Minor.
  WENDI. Ready, one, two, three.

(*All sing the first line of "House of the Rising Sun"; except JETTA, who pouts.*)

  WENDI. Sing, Jetta. Here's your mike. Are you gonna let us down? Think of Bev, think of Carol. Think of Larry. Do you want to spend the rest of your life ironing underwear? (*JETTA sings the second line.*)
  WENDI.
MAKE IT MEANER!!!! (*All sing the third line. They get into it as TIM enters, watching in disgust and disbelief.*)

  TIM. Mom!

---

*See cautionary note at bottom of p. 25.

BEV. Tim! AHHHH! (*They stop abruptly, hastily, awkwardly hiding their instruments.*)

TIM. What were you doing?

BEV. Nothing.

TIM. Mom, have you been doin the doob?

BEV. What do you mean?

TIM. Smoking marijuana.

BEV. No.

JETTA. We were practicing for a talent contest.

BEV. (*quickly*) For a make-up convention.

WENDI. Betty Jean stuff.

CAROL. Music to put make-up on by.

TIM. Cause it sounded like rock and roll. (*They all laugh somewhat loudly and nervously.*)

WENDI. Oh, haha, that's pretty funny, because we're a *Bluegrass* band!

TIM. With a marching drum?

CAROL. Yes, because we're a marching bluegrass band. We better get home, gals, and study those formations!

BEV. Carol, don't forget to go down to the "headquarters" and sign us up.

CAROL. Right. Bye. (*They exit quickly.*) Bye Tim, nice to see you.

TIM. What's wrong with them? Why did they leave so fast?

BEV. Just suddenly got tired I guess. You know — *old* people.

TIM. I didn't know you played guitar. Now we're *both* in a band.

BEV. (*suddenly interested in cleaning*) Um-hmm.

TIM. That's pretty funny.

BEV. (*to herself*) A lot funnier than you think.

BLACKOUT

SCENE 4

The bridge. WENDI is listening to punk music and practicing. WALLACE sneaks up behind her holding a teeny fish with no fins on a plaque. He touches it to her, she jumps.

WENDI. AHHHHH! Wallace, you scared me!

WALLACE. Sorry. Knock knock.

WENDI. Who's there?

WALLACE. Champ.

WENDI. Champ who.

WALLACE. Champ the winning fish!

WENDI. What happened to him? He looks weird.

WALLACE. It's the *fins*. I had them removed so I could laminate them and give them away as gifts. Great idea, huh?

WENDI. (*uninterested*) I guess. Wally, *wait* til you see the band. We're so funny! (*She resumes practicing.*)

WALLACE. (*equally uninterested*) Yeah, that's great! Are you coming down to the boat tonight?

WENDI. I can't, honey. We have to practice.

WALLACE. I knew this was going to happen. I'VE hung the drapes, painted the name on the stern, picked out the music. All you've done is install the rudder.

WENDI. That took me days.

WALLACE. Yeah, but I've still done three things to your one.

WENDI. Wallace, the whole world does not revolve around your boat.

WALLACE. Oh yeah? Are you forgetting that it was your idea to buy a sailboat and go to Hawaii in the first place.

WENDI. I'm not forgetting that, but this contest is important to me too.

WALLACE. More important than the trip, I guess.

WENDI. Not more important, but I could win $500.

WALLACE. I don't know why you need your own money. I pay for everything anyway.

WENDI. Now you're being petty.

WALLACE. I am *not* being *petty, you're* being *flakey.* You promised you'd help me work on the boat!

WENDI. Well, I'm sick of the boat!

WALLACE. What's come over you? Is it your time of the month or something?

WENDI. Ohh you . . . you boring dink.

WALLACE. Boring DINK? Boy Howdy am I glad I found out what a grouch you are before we got out on the boat and I woke up dead or something.

WENDI. And am I glad I found out what a nut you are. Laminated fish fins? Who wants 'em?

WALLACE. Betcha a lot of people would rather have a winning fish fin than watch you.

WENDI. Oh, go to hell!

WALLACE. That's it! I'm leaving.

WENDI. Good. And don't forget your stupid fish.

WALLACE. Don't you dare hurt Champ! He's *innocent!*

WENDI. He's stuffed! Get out!

WALLACE. I'm going!

WENDI. Good!

WALLACE. Just for that I'm taking back my I.D. bracelet, my favorite robe and all my Leonard Nimoy records. (*He exits angrily.*)

WENDI. Oh no, not the Leonard Nimoy records!

[MUSIC #5B: *WENDY-WALLACE PLAYOFF*]

(*Lights cut to BEV and TIM. BEV brings in two plates to the front room.*)

BEV. Tim, dinner! (*TIM enters, carrying his guitar.*)

TIM. Great, I'm starved. (*He sits on the couch and takes his plate, looking at it in disgust.*) Gross, macaroni again?

BEV. It's only the second time this week.

TIM. But it's the same junk we get in school.

BEV. I'm sorry, but it's all we can afford.

TIM. Least you could put hot dogs or something in it.

BEV. (*changing into her Clint Eastwood impression*) Hot dogs, you want hot dogs? I'll get you hot dogs. (*She exits leaving TIM to play with his food. She returns holding a full package of hotdogs.*) Hotdogs! (*She slams them onto his plate.*) There, happy? (*TIM looks at her in surprise as we go to JETTA and CAROL.*)

(*JETTA and CAROL are seated on two boxes and are whispering.*)

BOTH. (*singing*)

YOU THINK I AM YOUR SLAVE,
YOU THINK I AM YOUR SERVANT.

CAROL. It's hard to practice a punk song when you're whispering.

JETTA. But I don't want Larry to hear us.

CAROL. He can't hear us in the basement.

JETTA. Through the intercom he might.

CAROL. The intercom?!!

JETTA. Yes. He had one installed when we turned this into a rumpus room.

CAROL. You two have done wonders with this house.

JETTA. You know Larry, he likes the best of everything.

LARRY. (*entering with a flash light*) Jetta? Jetta!

JETTA. Over here behind the furnace, honey.

LARRY. This time I am *really* frosted. Now this is store bought grape juice. (*He holds a jar of juice in her face.*) You know I only like fresh squeezed. I can see now that we're going to have to revoke a few privileges around here. (*LARRY exits. JETTA stands sadly. CAROL nervously takes a sip of coffee.*)

CAROL. I don't care what he says about the grape juice. I still say you make the worlds best coffee.

JETTA. Thanks but Larry doesn't think so.

CAROL. (*sympathetically*) Oh, Jetta, is there something wrong between you two?

JETTA. I don't know Carol. (*She sings.*)

[MUSIC #6 *NOT AT HOME*]

MASTER BEDROOM WITH A BATH
LANDSCAPED GARDENS, SHADY PATH
CARPETING, AND FURNITURE AND DRAPES
  MATCH PERFECTLY

STAINED GLASS WINDOWS IN THE HALL
HARDWOOD FLOORS, I'VE GOT IT ALL
A PLACE FOR EVERYTHING AND NOTHING
OUT OF PLACE BUT ME.

OUR DREAM HOUSE ALL CAME TRUE
GOOD LOCATION, LOVELY VIEW
A HOME WITH EVERYTHING, EXCEPT A HEART
LIFE IS NEVER WHAT IT SEEMS
IN THE HOUSES OF OUR DREAMS
FOR WITHIN OUR DREAM HOUSE WE HAVE COME
  APART

I'M NOT AT HOME IN THE LIVING ROOM
I'M NOT AT HOME IN THE DINING ROOM
I'M NOT AT HOME ANYWHERE ANYMORE

I'M NOT AT HOME IN THE FAMILY ROOM
I'M NOT AT HOME IN THE BEDROOM
I'M NOT AT HOME, NOT AT HOME
IN MY OWN HOME

AS WE LIE IN BED AT NIGHT
BACK TO BACK, OUR BODIES TIGHT
WITH SILENT ANGER HANGING IN THE AIR
I MISS HIM VERY MUCH
AND I LONG TO FEEL HIS TOUCH
REMINDING ME THAT I BELONG SOMEWHERE

AND IN THE NIGHT I DREAM
THAT THE HOUSE COMES CRASHING DOWN
AND EVERYTHING WE OWN IS WASHED AWAY
HE AND I ARE LEFT
STANDING FACE TO FACE AT LAST
AND WE HAVEN'T GOT A SINGLE THING TO SAY

I'M NOT AT HOME IN THE LIVING ROOM
I'M NOT AT HOME IN THE DINING ROOM
I'M NOT AT HOME ANYWHERE ANYMORE

I'M NOT AT HOME IN THE FAMILY ROOM
I'M NOT AT HOME IN THE BEDROOM
I'M NOT AT HOME, NOT AT HOME
IN MY OWN HOME

CAROL. Gee, Jetta, I didn't know it was that bad.

JETTA. Thanks Carol. Larry and I are going to see a counselor. Maybe that'll help. I just don't want to get a divorce and end up like you.

BLACK OUT

[MUSIC #6A: *NOT AT HOME-PLAYOFF*]

SCENE 5

Lewd Fingers Club. LEWD is attempting to set the lights with an unseen tekkie named Weasel.

LEWD. Alright, Weasel, bring up the blues! (*Pink lights come up.*) No man, the other blues! (*Pinks go out, ambers come on.*) Weasel, blue lights B.L.E.U. n'est pas!? (*Ambers out, whites on.*) BLUE, BLUE, BLUE!!! *Blue* lights! Work *with* the drug, for chrissakes. (*blackout*) That's it! I'm gonna *kill* you, Weasel! (*He starts off.*)

(*CAROL enters and hears this, attempts to leave but can't find her way.*)

CAROL. Oh god!

LEWD. I think we got a prowler! (*LEWD feels his way in the dark, CAROL evades him.*) In fact, I *know* we got a prowler, I can smell spaghetti sandwiches. Weasel, give me some lights.

CAROL. AHHHHHH! HELP, HELP, HELP, HELP!

LEWD. What the hell? Calm *down!*

CAROL. Police, police, police!!!

LEWD. Hey, stop it! Calm down! Cool it.

CAROL. Let go of me! HHHEEEEEEEEEELLLPPPPP!!!!! (*She smacks him, he falls, lights come up, he holds his face.*)

LEWD. Hey, time out! Relax. Oww, why did you do that?

CAROL. I thought you were going to kill me.

LEWD. No, I was gonna kill Weasel. I thought you were going to rob me.

CAROL. Rob you? Of what?

LEWD. Ouchimama.

CAROL. Are you okay?

LEWD. Guess so. You play roller derby or something?

CAROL. No.

LEWD. You pack a pretty good punch.

CAROL. In High School I boxed.

LEWD. That explains it. So, like, what d'ya want?

CAROL. I came in to sign up for the contest tomorrow night.

LEWD. The punk contest? You're joking?!

CAROL. No, why?

LEWD. Cause usually people like you try to close us down, not play here.

CAROL. I don't want to close you down. I want my band to win the $2,000.

LEWD. Oh god, no sooner do we get a good fad going then the parents jump in and ruin it.

CAROL. No, you don't understand, I'm an Angry Housewife.

LEWD. Yeah, well—you and two million other women, you don't hear them singing about it.

CAROL. (*threatening him*) Look Pipsqueak, either you sign me or I'll pop you again.

LEWD. (*backing away*) Cool, cool. The name of your band is really The Angry Housewives?

CAROL. And it's got all women in it, got it??

LEWD. Alright, alright, I got it. You got five bucks? (*CAROL digs around in her purse.*)

CAROL. Do you take VISA?

LEWD. (*sarcastically*) Right.

CAROL. (*finally finds the cash*) Here you go. (*She gives it to him, he pockets it in his shoe.*) Can I have a receipt?

LEWD. A receipt? Sure. (*He writes on her palm.*) Five bucks to Lewd Fingers for contest. (*She giggles. He looks at her appreciatively.*) Hey, what's your name?

CAROL. (*shyly*) Carol.

LEWD. Carol. (*He savors the name.*) I'm Lewd. (*She takes a step back.*) Oh! Lewd *Fingers!* This is my club. I bet your boyfriend is lookin' forward to this.

CAROL. I'm, ah, sort of in between boyfriends right now.

LEWD. Me too.

CAROL. Oh. (*realizing he might be gay*) OH!

LEWD. No, I mean girlfriends.

CAROL. I see. Well, guess I better go. Big night tonight.

LEWD. I look forward to seein you! AND your band, of course.

CAROL. Me too. I mean I look forward to seeing you *and* your club. (*She begins to back out, accidently runs into a chair.*)

LEWD. Watch your step.

CAROL. I used to be a dancer. (*She trips again and exits.*)

LEWD. All right, Weasel. Let's try it again. The blues!

(*WALLACE enters.*)

WALLACE. Howdy do?

LEWD. You lost or something Bullwinkle? The moose lodge is across the street.

WALLACE. Is this a place called Lewd Fingers?

LEWD. Who wants to know?

WALLACE. See, my girlfriend's been acting really odd and she says she's playing in a band here tomorrow & . . .

LEWD. See any girls? See any band? Look I'm busy, so hoof it back to the K-Mart, nerd.

WALLACE. Alright. Pardon me, Tonto.

LEWD. Beat it.

WALLACE. Geez Louise!

LEWD. Geez Louise?

WALLACE. That's right.

LEWD. I haven't heard that in ages. Hey, your name isn't Wallace, is it?

WALLACE. (*nervous*) Maybe.

LEWD. Jollie, Ollie Wally?

WALLACE. No one's called me that since college.

LEWD. Don't you recognize me, man?

WALLACE. (*after staring at him a moment — then in surprise*) Conrad Michaels?!

LEWD. Yep!

WALLACE. The conman?

LEWD. The same!

BOTH. (*Wildly in joyful recognition, they do a fancy handshake.*)

X-AY, X-AY, X-AY HIGH
IS THE CHEER OF THEATA CHI!!!
WHOOOOA, WHOOOA, WHOOOA!

LEWD. Only my name is Lewd Fingers now and you're standin in my club. Where have you been all these years?

WALLACE. I recently won a million dollar fishing derby and. . . .

LEWD. Whoa, Jollie Ollie a millionaire.

WALLACE. And me and my, maybe still, girlfriend are sailin to Hawaii in my new sailing boat.

LEWD. I did some sailin in the 70's man, big turn on for the chicks.

WALLACE. Same old conman.

LEWD. Same old Wallie.

WALLACE. So, what about you? Last time I heard, you were living in a commune in San Francisco.

LEWD. Yeah well, I dropped out, then when that stopped makin' money, I dropped back in, then that stopped makin' money, so I dropped back out again — and here I am.

WALLACE. You're making money?

LEWD. You bet!

BOTH. Alright!

LEWD. So what's the name of your chick's band?

WALLACE. I don't know. It's a punk band.

LEWD. Of course it's a punk band. This is a punk club, for crissakes.

WALLACE. It's got all women in it.

LEWD. The Angry Housewives? This chick Carol just came in and signed them up. That your chick?

WALLACE. No she's my girlfriend's chick.

LEWD. She's pretty cute.

WALLACE. Same old Conrad, just like college. Boy it's been a long time.

[MUSIC #6: *BETSY MOBERLY*]

LEWD.
COLLEGE WAS GREAT
  WALLACE.
YEAH, VARSITY CREW
  LEWD.
SDS
  WALLACE.
DELTA MU, KEGGERS
  LEWD.
TEAR GAS
  WALLACE.
BALLGAMES
  LEWD.
RIOTS
  WALLACE.
ROTC
  LEWD.
PEACE
  WALLACE.
AND WOMEN
  LEWD.
MEN! NAH, JUST KIDDIN'
  BOTH.
WOMEN, WOMEN, WOMEN, YEAH WOMEN!
  WALLACE.
THE CARPENTERS

LEWD.
THE GRATEFUL DEAD
WALLACE.
ROSE BOWL
LEWD.
WOODSTOCK
WALLACE.
STREAKIN'
LEWD.
STRIKIN' GRASS
WALLACE.
BEER
LEWD.
MUSHROOMS
WALLACE.
BEER
LEWD.
PEYOTE
WALLACE.
BEER
LEWD.
ACID
WALLACE.
CHIVAS. . . . M.B.A.
LEWD.
P.H.D.
WALLACE.
REAL WORLD
LEWD.
AND PHILOSOPHY
BOTH.
AND WOMEN, WOMEN, WOMEN, YEAH. . . . WOMEN!
LEWD.
YOU KNOW I REMEMBER THE FIRST CHICK THAT
I. . . . . . . DATED
WALLACE.
YEAH, ME TOO
LEWD.
LET ME SEE, WHAT WAS HER NAME? BARBARA,
BETTY. . . . BETSY!
WALLACE.
BETSY! SO WAS MINE!

LEWD.
WOW, SYNCHRONICITY! THIS CHICK'S NAME WAS
    BETSY . . . BETSY
    WALLACE.
MOBERLY?
    LEWD.
YEAH, THAT'S IT
    WALLACE.
I WENT WITH BETSY MOBERLY TOO
    BOTH.
YOU MEAN YOU? OOOOH. HA HA HA HA HA HA HA
BETSY MOBERLY, WHAT DO YOU KNOW?
    LEWD.
WHAT A HEARTBREAKER
    WALLACE.
I HAVEN'T THOUGHT ABOUT HER IN YEARS
WHAT EVER HAPPENED TO BETSY MOBERLY?
THE GIRL MOST LIKELY TO
WHAT EVER HAPPENED TO BETSY MOBERLY?
NO ONE ON CAMPUS KNEW
SHE SAT BESIDE ME IN OCEANOGRAPHY
BUT SHE FLUNKED OUT ONE DAY
THAT WAS THE LAST TIME I SAW BETSY
THE GIRL WHO GOT AWAY
    LEWD.
GOOD OLD BETSY MOBERLY
GOOD OLD BETSY MOBERLY
SHE TAUGHT ME ALL I KNOW AND
SHE NEVER WORRIED ABOUT CONTRACEPTION

GOOD OLD BETSY MOBERLY
GOOD OLD BETSY MOBERLY
WAS EVERY FRESHMANS WET DREAM
AND I WAS NO EXCEPTION

SHE WAS WILD, SHE WAS FREE
BUT SHE DIDN'T CARE FOR ME
SO ONE DAY SHE CALLED ME UP TO SAY
GOODBYE, GOODBYE BABY
SHE WAS REALLY OUT OF SIGHT
AND I DREAMED OF HER AT NIGHT
GOOD OLD BETSY MOBERLY

WALLACE. Sorry!

WALLACE.   LEWD.

BACK
WOMEN WOMEN   DANCE BREAK

WALLACE.   LEWD.

WOMEN WOMEN   BETSY MOBERLY I
                                  REMEMBER HER

BETSY MOBERLY I
  REMEMBER HER

(*together*) WOMEN, WOMEN, WOMEN, WOMEN,
  WOMEN, . . . YEAH

WHAT EVER HAPPENED   GOOD OLD BETSY
  TO   MOBERLY

BETSY MOBERLY   GOOD OLD BETSY
                                   MOBERLY

THE GIRL MOST LIKELY   SHE TAUGHT ME ALL I
  TO . . .   KNEW AND SHE NEVER
                                 WORRIED ABOUT
                                 CONTRACEPTION

WHAT EVER HAPPENED   GOOD OLD BETSY
  TO   MOBERLY

BETSY MOBERLY   GOOD OLD BETSY
                                   MOBERLY

NO ONE ON CAMPUS   WAS EVERY FRESHMANS
  KNEW. . . .   WET DREAM AND I
                                 WAS NO EXCEPTION

SHE SAT BESIDE ME   SHE WAS WILD, SHE WAS
                                 FREE

IN OCEANOGRAPHY   BUT SHE DIDN'T CARE
                                 FOR ME

BUT SHE FLUNKED OUT   SO ONE DAY SHE
  ONE   CALLED ME UP
                                 TO SAY

DAY . . .   GOODBYE, GOODBYE
                                 BABY

THAT WAS THE LAST   SHE WAS REALLY OUT
  TIME   OF SIGHT

I SAW BETSY. . . .   AND I DREAMED OF HER
                                 AT NIGHT

BOTH.
THE GIRL WHO GOT AWAY

LEWD.
SHE GAVE ME BACK RUBS
BOTH.
THE GIRL WHO GOT AWAY
WALLACE.
WE SLEPT IN HOT TUBS
BOTH.
THE GIRL WHO GOT AWAY!!!!!!

LEWD. Hey, it was good seein ya man, but I gotta get set up for tomorrow, itsa big night. You comin? I'll put you on the guest list.

WALLACE. I'll be there. Say, you said you've sailed?

LEWD. Lots.

WALLACE. Maybe you could come on down to the boat, pound back a few brews and give me some pointers.

LEWD. You're sailin' to Hawaii and you don't know how?

WALLACE. (*slightly defensive*) I know most of it, I just have a few problems gettin the sails up and down is all.

LEWD. Sure, I'll help ya, for some bucks.

WALLACE. Same old conman.

LEWD. Same old Wally.

BOTH. (*same handshake as before*)
X-AY,X-AY,X-AY!!!!!!! (*WALLACE exits. LEWD goes back to his work.*)

LEWD. Alright Weasel, no excuses give me plenty of light. (*House goes to half. Warningly:*) WEASEL! (*blackout*) Shit.

SCENE 6

Lewd Fingers
The ANGRY HOUSEWIVES enter, stopping short of the stage and react to the reaction of the crowd to the other bands. They are drinking — heavily. They are, as promised, in punk drag — wigs, make-up, costumes, etc. They are also very scared.

CAROL. Do I look as stupid as I feel?

BEV. No, but *I* do.

JETTA. This sure helps. (*takes a long drink*)

BEV. Take that bottle away from Jetta.

CAROL. She's smashed.

WENDI. Just leave her alone, she'll be all right.

LEWD. All right. You girls ready? Let's go! Well, come *on*, let's go! (*into the microphone*) Stow it, mutants! First off, I want to thank K-R-A-P radio for sponsoring this event tonight. I want to remind you that the winner here tonight goes to the finals next week and a chance to win the grand prize of $4,000! And a recording contract. Comin' up next, we've got the last group of the evening — a totally rad, and way cool new band, the ANGRY HOUSEWIVES!! We got Brillo on the keyboards, Charmin on the drums, check out Stain on guitar, and Numzit as lead singer!! So here they are, The ANGRY HOUSEWIVES!! Take it away, girls! (*The spot focuses on Jetta, who is petrified. She does not move. LEWD takes the microphone to her. The crowd boos. LEWD drags JETTA to D.C.*) Get her singing or get her off the stage!

CAROL. She'll sing, already! She'll sing!

JETTA. What are they booing at?

WENDI. I don't know. Remember Clint Eastwood! Seething.

[MUSIC #7: *CORNFLAKES*]

JETTA. A-ONE, TWO, THREE, FOUR
  WOMEN.
AH

JETTA.	WOMEN.
WHERE DO YOU THINK YOU'RE GOIN?	EH
GET BACK IN HERE YOU TOADSTOOL	EH
YOU GOTTA EAT YOUR BREAKFAST	EH
BEFORE YOU GO TO HIGH SCHOOL	EH
YOU THINK I AM YOUR SLAVE	EH
YOU THINK I AM YOUR SERVANT	EH
I'VE FIXED YOUR FAVORITE CEREAL	EH
BUT YOU DO NOT DESERVE IT	
EAT YOUR FRIGGIN CORNFLAKES	EAT YOUR FRIGGIN CORNFLAKES

OR MOMMY WILL GET
MAD
EAT YOUR FRIGGING   EAT YOUR FRIGGIN
CORNFLAKES   CORNFLAKES
OR I'LL GO AND GET
YOUR DAD
YOU BETTER EAT THOSE   EH
CORNFLAKES
I'M LOSING PATIENCE   EH
HONEY
YOU BETTER EAT THOSE   EH
CORNFLAKES
THAT SHIT COSTS LOTSA   EH
MONEY
DON'T LEAVE THEM ON   EH
THE TABLE
THEY'LL GET SOGGY   EH
FOR GOD'S SAKE
FOR THE LAST TIME I'M
TELLING YOU
EAT YOUR FUCKING   EAT YOUR FUCKING
CORNFLAKES   CORNFLAKES
EAT YOUR FUCKING   DO WHAT MOMMY
CORNFLAKES   TELLS YOU
OR MOMMY WILL GET
MAD
EAT YOUR FUCKING   EAT YOUR FUCKING
CORNFLAKES   CORNFLAKES
                           DO WHAT MOMMY
                           TELLS YOU
OR I'LL GO AND GET   OR I'LL GO AND GET
YOUR DAD   YOUR DAD
(*An elevator rises with*   EH EH EH EH EH
CAROL, WENDY, and BEV   EH EH EH EH EH
on it. It is a giant Cornflakes
box.)

JETTA. (*pouring Cornflakes on the audience; spoke-sung over "Vamp"*)
IF YOUR LATE FOR SCHOOL, I'M NOT GOING TO
WRITE AN EXCUSE.
CHEW EVERY BITE 36 GODDAM TIMES

GRIND EM OR YOUR GROUNDED
EAT EM OR FUCKING WEAR EM

(She gets milk carton, drinks and pours confetti on the audience.)

ALL. EAT EM! EAT EM! EAT EM! EAT EM! EAT EM!
LEWD. And the winners are . . . THE ANGRY HOUSE-
WIVES!!! (*JETTA faints as the curtain falls.*)

END OF ACT I

ACT TWO

SCENE 1

Saturday Night — later
BEV's House
The lights come up. Screaming is heard offstage.

JETTA. I can't make it up your front steps!

BEV. I don't *have* any front steps!

ALL. Woops! (*ad lib WENDI enters.*)

CAROL. Jetta, let go of me! (*CAROL and JETTA enter, commotion/laughter.*)

WENDI. Will you hurry? Those guys looked dangerous! (*BEV enters. All are still in their punk costumes, and all but WENDI are in high form.*)

BEV. Oh stop being so silly, Wendi. They were just flirting with us.

WENDI. With their chains?

JETTA. (*very drunk*) Eat your fuckin' cornflakes!

WENDI. Jetta! Sit!

CAROL. Can you believe that Lewd Fingers asking me for my phone number?

BEV. You're kidding! Did you give it to him?

CAROL. (*a beat*) Yeah.

ALL. (*Ad lib negative responses to this news*)

CAROL. Well, he was *cute.*

BEV. This was so much fun! (*CAROL brings out a stack of bills and distributes them.*)

CAROL.
Okay everybody — here you go.
Five hundy for Bev.
Five hundy for Jetta
Five hundy FOR LIL' OL' ME
and finally A big five hundred to Wendi. (*Everyone cheers and screams except for WENDI.*)

BEV. The car is saved!! Wendi, you're brilliant!

WENDI. Oh, I don't know. I almost got my eye poked out by a mowhawk.

JETTA. Don't exaggerate.

WENDI. Thank God, that's over, huh??

47

CAROL. Over? Are you kidding? We're in the finals.

WENDI. But we did what we said we were going to do so we don't have to do the finals, right?! (*BEV, CAROL and JETTA stare at WENDI in disbelief. Inre, their stares*) I'm just asking.

BEV. We could win $4,000! It'll be so easy, those kids don't stand a chance. They all look the same.

JETTA. Alot of cute little fellars though.

WENDI. Jetta, you're drunk.

JETTA. (*takes another swig of champagne*) No, tough and seething.

CAROL. I can't believe I was ever their music teacher. They were *terrible!*

BEV. Weren't they? I thought *Tim's* band sucked the big one, but when I heard "Toe Jammin": (*BEV starts to imitate the song.*)

"TAKE OFF YOUR SHOES
NAH, NAH, NAH, NAH, NAH, NAH.
(*TIM enters unnoticed.*)
TAKE OFF YOUR SOCKS
NAH, NAH, NAH, NAH, NAH, NAH
SEE THE GUNK BETWEEN YOUR TOES."
(*She does a little dance step.*)

TIM. (*unable to stand it any more*) Mom!

BEV. (*to others, without missing a beat*) First, you marinate the beef. . . .

TIM. The Angry Housewives, huh? God, I feel so *stupid.*

BEV. I can explain.

TIM. (*Disgusted*) I saw you there and so did everyone else. A marching blue grass band!

BEV. Yeah! See, at the last minute we changed our minds.

CAROL. She did it for *you.*

JETTA. Timmy, don't be mad — you're so cute! (*JETTA staggers over to TIM, kisses him on the lips, and collapses in the corner.*)

TIM. Mom, if you go on to the finals, you'll ruin my life! (*Music intro starts.*)

BEV. What do you mean?

[MUSIC #8: *FIRST KID ON THE BLOCK*]

TIM.
I'M TOO YOUNG TO DIE

AND I'M TOO OLD TO CRY.
SO I GUESS I BETTER LEAVE TOWN.
'CAUSE THERE'S NO WAY I
CAN LOOK MY FRIENDS IN THE EYE
WHEN WORD STARTS GETTING AROUND
THAT MY MOM'S BAND BEAT MY BAND
AND, OH, IT EMBARRASSES ME
I NEVER THOUGHT I WOULD BE
THE FIRST KID ON THE BLOCK
TO HAVE A MOM IN PUNK ROCK.

WOMEN.
YA YA YA YA YA YA
YA YA YA YA YA YA
YA YA YA YA YA YA YA

TIM.
I GOTTA FIND A PLACE
WHERE I CAN HIDE MY FACE

WHEN THE KIDS CROWD ROUND MY LOCKER

I GOTTA RUN AWAY
CAUSE THEY'RE GONNA SAY

HEY I HEAR THAT YOUR MOM IS A ROCKER

IF MY MOM'S BAND
BEATS MY BAND
I'D BE SO HUMILIATED
SOMEHOW I NEVER THOUGHT I'D BE RATED

WOMEN.
OOH HOOP WHEE OO
OOH HOOP WHEE OO

OOH OOH OOH SHA LA

OOH HOOP WHEE OO
OOH HOOP WHEE OH

LA LA OOH WAH

WAH
WAH
WAH AH OOH
AH HAH OOO LA LA

BA DA DA

THE FIRST KID ON THE BLOCK
TO HAVE A MOM IN PUNK ROCK

THE FIRST KID ON THE BLOCK
TO HAVE A YA YA YA
YA YA YA
YA YA YA YA YA YA
YA YA YA YA YA YA
YA YA YA YA YA YA YA

TOTAL TRAVESTY
AND I FEEL SO RETARDED

OOH OOH OOH OOH SHA LA

IF IT WAS ANYONE OTHER THAN MY OWN MOTHER	OOH HOOP WHEE OO (2X)
I WOULDN'T BE SO BROKEN HEARTED	LA LA OOH WAH
BUT MY MOM'S BAND	WAH
COULD BEAT MY BAND	WAH
AND I FEEL SO REJECTED	WAH AH OOH
SOMEHOW I JUST NEVER EXPECTED TO BE	AH HAH LA LA LA BA DA DA

ALL.
THE FIRST KID ON THE BLOCK
THE FIRST KID ON THE BLOCK
THE FIRST KID ON THE BLOCK
TO HAVE A

TIM.	WOMEN.
MOM	YA YA YA YA YA
	YA YA YA YA YA
IN PUNK ROCK	YA YA YA YEAH
	OOO WEE OOO OOO

AY YAI YAI YAI YAI
WOMEN.
RING RING RING
TIM.
HELLO
WOMEN.
HI TIM THIS IS SUZIE
TIM.
OH WOW, HI SUZIE
WOMEN.
IS YOUR MOM HOME?
TIM.
NO! SHE'S NOT!
WOMEN.
AHHHH! SHE'S SO NEAT!
TIM.
DAMMIT!

	WOMEN.
MY LIFE WILL BE A TOTAL TRAVESTY	OOH HOOP WHEE OO (2X)

I FEEL SO RETARDED.
IF IT WAS SOME ONE OTHER
THAN MY OWN MOTHER
I WOULDN'T BE SO BROKEN-HEARTED.
FOR MY MOM'S BAND BEAT MY BAND.
AND I FEEL SO DEJECTED.
SOMEHOW I JUST NEVER EXPECTED
TO BE THE FIRST KID ON THE BLOCK
THE FIRST KID ON THE BLOCK
I'LL BE THE FIRST KID ON THE BLOCK
TO HAVE A MOM IN PUNK ROCK.
    ALL.
OOO-EE-OO-OO.

(*TIM ends the song holding his head in shame.*)

BEV. Don't be so dramatic.
TIM. How can I show my face in school?
BEV. Don't admit I'm your mother.
TIM. You're not. A mother who loved me wouldn't do this.
CAROL. Don't let him do this to you. Fight it.
BEV. (*fighting the onslaught of guilt*) I . . . am NOT. . . .
going. . . . to. . . . stop!
TIM. And all this time I was so worried about you, thinking that
you were on drugs.
BEV. Oh Tim, what kind of mother do you think I am?
TIM. An *ex*-mother. I'm an orphan. (*TIM stomps off to his
room.*)
BEV. (*going after him*) Tim, wait!
CAROL. (*grabbing BEV*) Let him go, he's just manipulating
you.
JETTA. (*still in the corner*) The little brat, kids are all alike.

(*TIM enters with a large Teddy Bear.*)

BEV. Where are you going?
TIM. To Ziggy's. I hope you sleep well tonight. His house has
rats.
BEV. Tim! Don't leave. This is the most fun I've had since your
father died. I mean . . .
TIM. You're ruining my life! Now I'll probably grow up and get
into all sorts of things, drugs, booze, WHITE SUGAR! (*BEV
collapses into CAROL's arms.*)

CAROL. Bev, be strong!

BEV. Tim . . . I'm sorry but you're just going to have to deal with it.

TIM. Fine, give me a ride to Ziggy's.

BEV. No!

TIM. Give me ten for a cab.

BEV. No.

TIM. Okay, I'll walk. But remember this. You're going to look really bad in my autobiography. (*TIM exits, BEV starts to follow but is stopped by CAROL.*)

CAROL. He'll be back, don't worry.

WENDI. All right. I really think we should rethink this band thing. Tim's mad at you, Wally's mad at me, and when *Larry* finds out. . . .

JETTA. I'm going to tell Larry what he can do with his corporate image. (*trying to stand*)

WENDI. Don't do it. It's just not worth it.

BEV. You're saying it's not worth it now after what I've just done?

CAROL. Wendi, if you back out, I'll kill you.

WENDI. What?

JETTA. (*falling down*) Tonight, *I'm* going to kill *Larry.*

WENDI. I better get Jetta home.

CAROL. (*dangerously*) See you at rehearsal tomorrow — *right?*

WENDI. Right, right.

JETTA. Bye! I don't feel very good. But I had a really good time tonight. See you! (*WENDI drags JETTA out.*)

BEV & CAROL. Bye, Jetta.

CAROL. You had a real breakthrough, Bev?

BEV. (*trying to be brave*) Thanks. It was time to cut those apron strings anyway. (*crumbling*) My Baby!!!!!!

BLACKOUT

[MUSIC 9A: *FIRST KID PLAYOFF*]

SCENE 2

A freeway overlook.
CAROL & LEWD are eating french fries.

CAROL. So this is your favorite view, huh?

LEWD. Oh yeah, I love the freeway at rush hour. It's a great place to see the sunset. French fry? (*He puts french fry in his mouth and they share it. They each eat on the end till they meet in the middle and kiss.*)

CAROL. Got any ketchup?

LEWD. You're really out there, you know?

CAROL. I am?

LEWD. Here you are, a mature woman playin' in a *band!* You got spunk, you're gutsy, I like that.

CAROL. But I didn't used to be like this. I was married, I played bridge, I was a member of the PTA.

LEWD. Please Carol, I don't need to hear about your sordid past. All that matters is that I like what I see now.

CAROL. Really?

[MUSIC #10: *LOVE-O-METER*]

LEWD.
I GOT MYSELF A LITTLE LOVE-O-METER
BEATIN HERE INSIDE OF MY CHEST
AND I JUST CHECK IN WITH MY LOVE-O-METER
TO FIND THE KIND OF STUFF I LIKE THE VERY BEST
I LIKE HALLOWEEN
SPIKES AND CHAINS
RIDIN ALL NIGHT ON COMMUTER TRAINS
BUT WHEN YOU HOLD ME HONEY MY LOVE-O-METER
    HITS THE TOP
AND WHEN YOU SQUEEZE ME HONEY HANG ON
    SLOOPY NEVER STOP
AND WHEN YOU KISS ME KISS ME KISS ME LITTLE
    DARLIN I STAY KISSED
YOU BROKE THE NEEDLE ON MY LOVE-O-METER
YOU'RE NUMBER ONE ON MY LIST
    CAROL.
I KNOW ABOUT YOUR LITTLE LOVE-O-METER
CAUSE LITTLE DARLIN I GOT ONE TOO
BUT I DON'T NEED TO CHECK MY LOVE-O-METER
TO KNOW EXACTLY WHAT I FEEL FOR YOU
I LOVE SARAH LEE, MALLOMARS
CLIPPIN OUT COUPONS FOR CANDY BARS
BUT WHEN YOU HOLD ME DARLIN MY LOVE-O-

METER HITS THE TOP
AND WHEN YOU SQUEEZE ME HONEY HANG ON
    SLOOPY NEVER STOP
AND WHEN YOU KISS ME KISS ME KISS ME LITTLE
    DARLIN I STAY KISSED
YOU BROKE THE NEEDLE ON MY LOVE-O-METER
    Lewd.
MY LIFE WAS SWEET BUT NOW MY LIFE IS SWEETER
    Both.
YOU BROKE THE NEEDLE ON MY LOVE-O-METER
YOU'RE NUMBER ONE ON MY LOVE LIST
    Lewd.
NUMBER ONE
    Carol.
NUMBER ONE
    Both.
ON MY LIST

Carol. What's your name?

Lewd. My real name? Conrad Michaels the Third!

Carol. Where'd you get Lewd Fingers?

Lewd. Practice.

Carol. Lewd, do you think we really have a chance at this contest?

Lewd. You have a great chance!

Carol. How do you know?

Lewd. (*counting on his fingers*) 1. You've got a great concept. 2. I'm an entrepreneur—I know talent. 3. Besides it's my club, I pick the judges.

[MUSIC 10A: *SCENE CHANGE #1*]

(*Cut to BEV's. She's obviously been up all night worrying. When TIM enters she pretends to be engrossed in the guitar.*)

Tim. (*sheepishly*) Hi mom.

Bev. (*hiding her relief*) Tim. You're back!

Tim. Yeah, I had a fight with Ziggy, so I punched him and came home.

Bev. You punched him?

Tim. He kept calling your band the Middle Aged Spreads. I had to hit him.

Bev. Is he hurt?

Tim. No. Kinda broke up our band though.

BEV. I'm sorry, honey.

TIM. Oh well, that's show biz. How's the guitar playing going?

BEV. Just okay.

TIM. I'll help you.

BEV. You will?

TIM. Sure, it'll be something we can do together. And I've been thinking, I figure we could make a lot of money with your band off fan club dues.

BEV. A fan club? But what would they get out of it?

TIM. Tours of the house, autographed pictures, stuff like that.

BEV. But what if we lose?

TIM. You can't, mom. I've hired a lawyer and set up a limited partnership with me and your band. If you love me, you'll sign. (*Taking out a contract, BEV is shocked.*)

[MUSIC 10B: *SCENE CHANGE #2*]

(*Cut to LARRY and JETTA's. LARRY is in the shower, then JETTA dresses him.*)

LARRY. (*off*) You're *what?*

JETTA. Playing in a punk rock band. (*LARRY enters in a towel and shower cap.*) Now honey, it's not that bad.

LARRY. Not that bad? I'll be the laughing stock of the entire firm.

JETTA. (*patting him dry*) They won't know.

LARRY. (*as JETTA hands him his robe*) They're already snickering because I had to pick up Annette three times this week. (*JETTA hands him a pair of boxer shorts.*)

JETTA. I could win $500.00! (*LARRY puts on the shorts.*)

LARRY. I give you an allowance.

JETTA. But it's more than just the money, there's the excitement.

LARRY. BUT — you have a job to do and that job is to take care of me and Annette, *my* job is to provide for you. (*He sits in a chair as JETTA puts his socks on.*)

JETTA. But I think there's more to life than that.

LARRY. Well of course, there's Scrabble Games. Why don't you do something normal like knit sweaters or glue pictures on wood?

JETTA. (*standing, garnering her strength*) But I like this punk band.

LARRY. (*laughs*) No you don't. (*He sits her down.*) I know you're a little disappointed but there's no way any wife of mine is going to disgrace me by prancing around on stage. Capiche?

JETTA. I guess you're right. Gee, and I was having so much fun, too.

LARRY. (*pats her head*) Tell you what. After we're finished grooming me, and after you've given the news to the girls, let's go for a ride to the board of trade. Would you like that?

JETTA. (*with feigned cheerfulness*) Yeah, that sounds like fun. (*JETTA starts to exit but changes her mind.*) Actually, Larry, that sounds really boring.

LARRY. We don't have to go anywhere if that's your attitude.

JETTA. And I'm not going to call the girls.

LARRY. Jetta, I'm warning you, don't make me sweat.

JETTA. I'm sorry Larry, no I'm not sorry. I think it's time I did something on my own.

LARRY. (*as his legs shake*) Oh no, now you made my leg twitch. Think about my clients.

JETTA. Oh, poop on your clients.

LARRY. POOP on my clients?!!

JETTA. Your wife is doing important things too.

LARRY. AAHHH!! My lips are chapping! What has come over you?

JETTA. Nothing, honey—at least let me tell you why it's so important.

LARRY. I don't want to hear. (*He plugs his ears and sings "Twinkle, Twinkle Little Star."*)

JETTA. Please don't sing. Besides we can't quit it's in the papers.

LARRY. The papers! Ow, my eyebrows feel like they're on fire.

JETTA. Oh and it's really fun, sweetie. We have this funny song: Eat Your Frigging Cornflakes.

LARRY. THAT . . . is the disguised "F" word. Now my toes are throbbing.

JETTA. And Lewd Fingers says . . .

LARRY. (*the final straw*) AHHH!! Oh God, I've got to go to the bathroom (*LARRY runs, with knees together, offstage. Cut to a park scene.*)

(*WENDI is sitting, downcast, on a park bench. After a beat, WALLY enters, spots WENDI.*)

[MUSIC #11: *SATURDAY NIGHT* Intro-underscore]

WALLACE. Wendi!

WENDI. Wally!

WALLACE. I've been looking all *over* for you.

WENDI. You have? I thought I'd never see you again. I missed you.

WALLACE. I missed you too.

BOTH. About that fight . . .

WALLACE. It was my fault.

WENDI. No, no — it was my fault.

WALLACE. No it wasn't, it was mine.

WENDI. Mine!

WALLACE. Mine!!!!

WENDI. WALLACE IT WAS MY FAULT!!!!!

WALLACE. Why does it always get to be *your* fault? (*WENDI groans in frustration and moves away. WALLACE grabs her.*) Okay, okay it was your fault.

WENDI. Oh, Wally! (*They hug. WALLACE breaks the embrace.*)

WALLACE. Congrats on that review, Wendi!

WENDI. What review? Where?

WALLACE. In Bleeding Ear Magazine! You haven't seen it? (*He pulls it out of his pocket and reads.*) "Far and away the most exciting band to emerge from Saturday's contest was the Angry Housewives!!! The four woman group with a style all their own stunned the crowd at Lewd Fingers. Lead singer Num . . . Num . . ." (*He can't pronounce it.*)

WENDI. Numzit.

WALLACE. "Numzit, screamed like a banshee, hurling motherly abuse at the underaged crowd." (*WENDY grabs the magazine and throws it on the ground.*)

WENDI. I don't want to hear anymore.

WALLACE. Hey, I was going to save that!

WENDI. Why?!

WALLACE. Cause I thought you guys were great!

WENDI. You were there? Why didn't you say anything?

WALLACE. I don't know, I guess I was afraid you wouldn't want to see me.

WENDI. I would have been so much happier if you'd been there.

WALLACE. I brought you a present Wendi. Sort of a "forgive me" gift.

WENDI. What is it?

WALLACE. Close your eyes. (*She does and WALLACE brings out a fish fin on a chain. He digs a necklace out of his pocket with a laminated fishfin on it and holds it in front of her face.*) Okay! Open them up! (*She is naturally startled.*)

WENDI. What is it?

WALLACE. Laminated fishfin! Yeah, I know, you think it's stupid. But it's good luck.

WENDI. Oh, I'm sorry I said it was dumb. It's sweet. Oh Wally!

WALLACE. Is something wrong?

WENDI. We have to play again.

WALLACE. Yeah, I know. But, don't worry about the trip. I understand. A chance like this comes once in a lifetime — like me and the derby.

WENDI. Wallace, listen to me. I don't want to play again. I want to go on the trip with you.

WALLACE. With me? You want to go on the trip with me?

WENDI. Yeah.

WALLACE. No, I'm gonna have to be the man here and say, "No way."

WENDI. What?

WALLACE. Now Wendi, it's for your own good. I don't want to hear 30 years from now, "I could have been a punk rock star, but I went off with you."

WENDI. I would never say that. Wallace, the whole time I was out there, all I could think was, when are we gonna get off the stage. All those kids screaming at us — it was horrible.

WALLACE. You'll get used to it.

WENDI. I don't want to get . . . Did you see what we were wearing? I couldn't believe myself.

WALLACE. I thought you looked sexy.

WENDI. You did? Well, I felt stupid.

WALLACE. Well, how do the others feel about playing again?

WENDI. They're thrilled about it. And I have to tell them today I'm not going to do it.

WALLACE. They're not gonna be very happy about that.

WENDI. Well, I know, but I've been trying really hard all week. We've been working on this new song and I just hate it. I get sick thinking about it.

WALLACE. You're the one that put 'em up to this, you know.

WENDI. You're the one who thought it was a dumb idea, now you want me to do it?

WALLACE. You're the one who thought it was a great idea, now you don't want to do it?

WENDI. I don't want to talk about it any more. My mind is made up, and besides, I'm late. I have to meet 'em for dinner.

WALLACE. You've been friends a long time. I hope you know what you're doing.

WENDI. Well, you know, I think they'll understand. Anyway, maybe they've changed their minds too. I don't want to talk about it. (*WENDI escapes to another part of the stage. WALLACE sings.*)

SATURDAY NIGHT

WALLACE.
MY GIRLFRIEND'S THE DRUMMER
SAYS DRUMMING'S A BUMMER
AND NOW SHE WANTS TO DROP OUT.
SHE'D RATHER BE SAILING
SHE'D RATHER BE SAILING
OH, WENDI WHAT A COP OUT.
BUT OKAY WITH ME
IF THAT'S THE WAY SHE WANTS TO BE.
SHE OUGHT TO FEEL GOOD
CAUSE SHE COULD BE REAL GOOD
BUT I'D RATHER NOT FIGHT.
BUT I KNOW THAT SHE COULD GET IT RIGHT
ON SATURDAY—
WENDY, CAROL, BEV.
NIGHT.

CAROL/BEV	WENDI
OH GOD, WHAT HAVE I GOT MYSELF INTO?	I JUST DON'T WANT TO DO THIS.
OH GOD, WHAT HAVE I I GOT MYSELF INTO?	I REALLY HATE THIS.

WENDY/CAROL/BEV.
MAYBE WE SHOULD CANCEL
IT DOESN'T FEEL RIGHT
IF ONLY WE WERE YOUNGER
WE MIGHT, WE MIGHT
HAVE THE CHANCE TO GET IT RIGHT.
ON SATURDAY NIGHT.
LEWD/TIM AND JETTA. (*who sings to herself*)
YOU'RE NERVOUS, YOU SHOW IT.
YOU'RE NERVOUS, DON'T BLOW IT.

COME ON NOW, YOU'RE A MESS.
RELAX, ENJOY AND DON'T DESTROY
YOUR CHANCES FOR SUCCESS
   Lewd,Tim, and Jetta.
GO WASH YOUR HAIR
GO SAY A PRAYER
GO BRUSH YOUR TEETH
GO REST.
YOU KNOW YOU'RE TALENTED
IT'S GONNA BE ALRIGHT
YOU'RE GONNA KNOCK 'EM DEAD.
YOU KNOW YOU'RE GONNA GET IT RIGHT
ON SATURDAY NIGHT!!!
   Larry.
MY WIFE IS BEING KIDNAPPED
BY THE ANGRY HOUSEWIVES
MY MARRIAGE COULD BE UP AGAINST THE WALL.
SHE WANTS TO BE A MEMBER OF THE
ANGRY HOUSEWIVES.
A GROUP THAT I DON'T UNDERSTAND AT ALL.
WHY DOES SHE FEEL THAT SHE ISN'T LIVING?
SHE THREATENING MY CORPORATE CLIMB.
WHAT DOES SHE WANT THAT I HAVEN'T GIVEN
MORE BABIES, MORE CREDIT CARDS—
MORE ORGASMS?
WE LIVE IN A PERILOUS TIME!
SHE WANTS TO BE A MEMBER OF THE ANGRY
   HOUSEWIVES
AND I DON'T UNDERSTAND IT AT ALL.
   All.
SING THEIR VERSES TOGETHER.

   Larry. There you go Annette. Drink your little bottle while daddy gets ready for only the most important lunch in his entire career! That's it, sweetie. (*He puts on a tie. He calls:*) Jetta? Shoot. Annette, how does this tie look? (*Baby cries.*) I thought you liked this tie, Trip Simington gave it to me. Uncle Tripper? (*Baby still cries.*) All right, all right. How about this one? (*Baby cries.*) You're right, too loud. This one? (*Baby cries.*) Golly sakes! What do you want from me? (*He wipes his face with the apron. The crying stops. He removes the apron. The crying starts. He covers his face, the crying stops. He uncovers his face, the crying begins.*) Very funny Annette. We'll see about that new car when you're sixteen. (*He starts to tie the tie.*) Right over left? Left over right? How does Jetta tie these things?

(*He dials the phone. Lights up on TIM.*)

TIM. Hello, — Angry Housewives Headquarters.

LARRY. Headquarters? Is this Bev's house?

TIM. Yeah. Wanna buy a tee-shirt?

LARRY. No. I would like to speak to my wife Jetta. Is she there?

TIM. No, she took my mom and them out to celebrate.

LARRY. Celebrate what?

TIM. The Angry Housewives. Where've you been man?

LARRY. I can't believe they're doing this.

TIM. I can't believe all the money that's pouring in from the fan club.

LARRY. What fan club?

TIM. The Angry Housewives Fan Club. We've got tee shirts, buttons, tours of the house. Stuff like that.

LARRY. Tours of the house? Look, do you know where she took them?

TIM. Yeah. Bone Poison. It's a restaurant. Some foreign place.

LARRY. Bone Poison? Bon Poisson! I have a business account there!

BLACK OUT

SCENE 3

[MUSIC #11A: *COCKTAIL MUSIC*]

The Bon Poisson Restaurant, BEV, CAROL, and JETTA are sitting and having champagne and hors d'ouevres. Tasteful cocktail piano is playing.

BEV. Jetta, this is a wonderful place! Are you sure you can afford this?

JETTA. Oh sure, no problem. Larry's firm has a business account here. Besides, I wanted to celebrate.

BEV. What are we celebrating?

JETTA. I stood up to Larry.

CAROL. You did? What happened?

JETTA. I told him about our band and he said the "F" word. Then he went to his mother's. But before he left he shook my hand! He only shakes hands with clients he's impressed with. So I wanted to celebrate. If it weren't for you guys I'd never have done it.

BEV. A toast to Jetta's new-found independence, and to the Angry Housewives.

ALL. The Angry Housewives! GRRR!

JETTA. There's Wendi. (*They all holler and wave.*)

BEV. Partay!

WENDI. Shhhh! Everyone is looking!

JETTA. Don't be such a weenie.

WENDI. I have to talk to you guys.

CAROL. Why not? That's what friends are for.

WENDI. I know you guys are excited about the band and all, but I think we should think of a better way to make money.

CAROL. What's wrong with the punk band?

WENDI. That was a stupid idea. We need one that's not as dangerous.

JETTA. It isn't dangerous.

WENDI. It is too. Do you remember when they threw bottles at the bands they didn't like, and spit cokes at the bands they *did* like?

JETTA. I thought that was funny.

WENDI. That's not the point.

CAROL. What is the point, Wendi?

WENDI. That there is a much safer and saner way to make money. Right? Right? Great! Let's drink to a great idea but a bad reality.

CAROL. We are going through with the punk band, Wendi.

WENDI. Are you crazy? We won't win.

BEV. And why not?

WENDI. Because what's in right now is sexy tough boys and girls in ripped leather jackets — not sophisticated women like ourselves.

CAROL. No one has ever accused *me* of being sophisticated. I think you're doing what you always do.

WENDI. What's that?

CAROL. Changing your mind at the last minute.

WENDI. You don't understand.

CAROL. I understand that you've done this to us so many times I've lost count.

WENDI. Don't exaggerate!

CAROL. What about that time we went to the amusement park and you talked us into going on that upside down ride?

BEV. That's right! *We* all got on. The ride started and you were watching us from the ground.

WENDI. There was no room in the car.

BEV. We were the only ones on the ride, Wendi.

JETTA. Yeah, I remember because Bev puked on my shoe and Carol had to be taken away on a stretcher.

CAROL. And how about the blood drive you talked us into? Everyone gave blood but you.

WENDI. They wouldn't take my blood.

BEV. They couldn't find your blood, Wendi. You hid under the table. I can't believe you suckered us in again.

JETTA. I can't believe I've wasted my first fight with Larry on something that won't even happen.

WENDI. Then go ahead, get up there and look stupid — but you're gonna have to find another drummer.

CAROL. We CAN'T! The contest is *tomorrow night!* We *don't have time!* (*The music stops abruptly. They clap politely.*)

WENDI. I'm sorry, you guys. You're upset now, but think about it and you'll realize I'm right.

JETTA. You know, Wendi, you're a creep.

BEV. You'll never make it to Hawaii, you'll probably jump ship half way.

JETTA. Quitter!

WENDI. Oh, real nice! I'm the only one with problems? Carol, you don't even deal with your problems, you just shovel food in your face! And Jetta can't even make a left hand turn without a written note from Larry. And Bev . . . Tim's turned into Godzilla because. . . .

BEV. How dare you! Tim's a great kid now.

JETTA. Larry has *never* written me a note. . . . for driving.

CAROL. That's okay ladies, she's just feeling guilty.

WENDI. Will you listen? I'm just trying to make a point. (*accidentally tosses food on CAROL*)

CAROL. (*tossing it back*) So was that.

WENDI. That was an accident. (*tosses it back, it hits BEV*)

BEV. This is dryclean! How does that feel? (*She deliberately throws some food on WENDI*)

WENDI. (*shocked*) Carol started it! (*tosses some on CAROL*)

CAROL. Oh yeah? (*tosses it back*)

WENDI. Yeah!! (*tosses it but it hits BEV*)

BEV. Wendi, how immature! (*throws some on WENDI*)

JETTA. Ladies, please!

WENDI. Why don't you guys grow up.

CAROL. Why don't *we* grow up?

JETTA. Yeah — *you're* the baby.

BEV. Let's go, girls. We'll find another drummer.

WENDI. But . . . but, listen you guys. . . .

CAROL. There are hundreds of women out there who play drums.

JETTA. I'm never listening to you again. Ready, Angry Housewives? (*They, exit angrily.*)

WENDI. Wait! What about the check? (*She sits, takes a drink.*) Good, find another drummer. See if I care.

(*LARRY enters quickly with his tie mis-tied.*)

LARRY. Hi, Wendi. Wendi! Where's Jetta? I gotta talk her out of this punk band, it's driving me nuts.

WENDI. I wouldn't do that if I were you. I just tried.

LARRY. You tried? I thought it was your idea?

WENDI. It was, but I changed my mind. It was stupid.

LARRY. It IS stupid.

WENDI. They didn't think so. They got so mad at me we had a food fight.

LARRY. A food fight? Here? On my business account? (*She starts to leave.*) Where are you going? Sit back down.

WENDI. Why, do you want to throw food at me too?

LARRY. No, I want to talk about this punk band.

WENDI. Larry, all I have been talking about is this punk band. I don't want to talk about it anymore. I have to think about it. Have some champagne, Larry. It's on you. (*She exits.*)

LARRY. They couldn't have a food fight with domestic champagne? C'mon world . . . dump on old Lare some more. (*He pours four glasses of champagne and drinks each between lines. To an unseen customer:*) What are you lookin at Bug Eyes!!?? First I lose my wife to a punk band. (*drinks*)
Then my own mommy kicks me out. (*drinks*)
Then I get stuck for the tab for my wife's food fight. (*drinks*)
Why is this happening to me? (*He drinks from the bottle.*)

[MUSIC #12: *NOBODY LOVES ME*]

IT ISN'T FAIR, IT ISN'T RIGHT
WELL I WAS BLIND BUT NOW I FIND
I'M BEGINNING TO SEE THE LIGHT
LOOK WHAT HAPPENS TO YOU:
YOU GO YOUR WAY, FROM DAY TO DAY
YOU GET ALONG WITH EVERYONE
IN YOUR USUAL NIFTY WAY
THEN THEY STICK IT TO YOU

THEY'RE ALWAY NICE AS PIE TILL THERE'S A CRISIS
THEN THE WOMAN WHO TIES YOUR TIES IS
TURNING AROUND AND TURNING ON YOU
WOO WOO WHAT'S A PERSON SUPPOSED TO DO
Know what?
THEY STAB YOUR BACK, AND TWIST THE BLADE
ALTHOUGH YOU'RE SWELL, THEY GIVE YOU HELL
FOR EVERY LITTLE MISTAKE YOU'VE MADE
Know why?
THEY THINK YOU'LL COME CRAWLING BACK AND
    APOLOGIZE
CRAWLIN BACK WITH TEARS IN YOUR EYES
BEGGIN WONT YA TREAT ME LIKE YOU DID BEFORE
What kind of guy falls for a trick like that? A jerk! Do I look like a
jerk? I'm not a jerk. Ask anybody, they'll tell ya. Ask my
boss. . . . no don't ask my boss. Ask my mommy. . . . no don't
ask my mommy. Ask my wife. . . . Jetta. . . . she'll tell
ya . . . I'm a jerk.
I WASN'T KIND, I WASN'T BRIGHT
I WAS BLIND BUT NOW I FIND
I'M BEGINNING TO SEE THE LIGHT
What a doo-doo I've been.
I NEVER CALLED, I SHOULD HAVE PHONED
I BETTER BEND AND MAKE AMENDS
OR SPEND THE REST OF MY LIFE ALONE. . . .
Alone.
I BETTER GO CRAWLIN BACK ON MY HANDS AND MY
    KNEES
AND BEGGIN PLEASE HONEY PLEASE
TAKE ME BACK AND LOVE ME LIKE YOU DID BEFORE

I CAN'T TAKE IT, I JUST CAN'T TAKE IT
CAUSE NOBODY LOVES ME ANY MORE

NOBODY LOVES ME ANYMORE

BLACKOUT

SCENE 4

*Lewd Fingers Club. The club is in full roar. LEWD enters
in full punk garb.*

LEWD. All right. All right. That was Big Dick and His Privates,
singing Please Be Hard On Me. Now before we get on with our big
bad battle of the bands, I have a few announcements to make.
Now the police have asked me to tell you that whoever gave their
dope sniffin dog a mowhawk is in deep shit. Whoever has the VW
license plate HELL get it out of the ladies can, the lines are bad
enough already. I want to thank KRAP radio for sponsoring
tonight's event. Thank you, Krap. Now our final band of the
evening is the Angry Housewives. . . . but unfortunately,
they've run into a little bad luck. Their drummer
is . . . uh . . . dead. But it's cool cause I'm sittin' in for her.
So, ladies and gentlemen . . . I give you the Angry
Housewives!!!!!!

[MUSIC PRE 13: *BEFORE STALLING FOR TIME*]

(*WALLACE enters dressed as WENDI in punk drag.*) Wendi?

WALLACE. No it's me, Wallace. I'm sitting in for Wendi.
LEWD. Forget it, I got it covered. (*into mike*) The Angry
Housewives!!!!!!!

(*TIM enters dressed like a girl.*)

LEWD. Who the hell are you?
TIM. It's me, Tim. I'm sittin in for Wendi. (*WALLACE and
TIM ad lib to each other. Crowd is screaming.*)
LEWD. (*into mike*) Shut your cakeholes! The Angry
Housewives!!!!!!

(*LARRY enters dressed as a woman*)

LARRY. (*yelling as he enters*) Watch it! Listen, punk, I'm a
lawyer and I'm gonna call myself in the morning.

LEWD. Who are you, tootsie?

LARRY. I'm sitting on Wendi.

LEWD. Great, four drummers and no band. (*ad libs as LEWD
is called by Weasel*)

LEWD. Beautiful—they're nowhere to be found. We're in
trouble here. (*into mike*) Okay! I got a special treat for you
here. . . . a Reggae band from New Zealand. . . . the uh. . . .
Coyote Uglies. They're gonna back me up on a number called
Stalling For Time.

LARRY. I don't know Reggae.

LEWD. Wing it or die! Three. Two. One. Zero.

[MUSIC #13: *STALLING FOR TIME*]

ALL.
LEWD FINGERS
WOH-OH-OH UH-UH-UH YA!
GO LEWD FINGERS
LEWD.
STALLING FOR TIME
WOH OH OH
STALLING FOR TIME
WOH OH OH
LARRY.
AND I
WALLY.
AND I
TIM.
AND I
ALL.
AM STALLING FOR TIME
LARRY.
DAY OH
LEWD.
IMPROVISING
ALL.
YOU'RE CRAZY
LEWD.
TREADING WATER

ALL.
OH BABY
  LEWD.
AND I
  LARRY.
AND I
  WALLY.
AND I
  TIM.
AND I
  ALL.
AM STALLING FOR TIME
  LARRY.
DAY-OH
  LEWD.
RASTAMAN
  ALL.
HURRY UP HOUSEWIVES AHHHH
  LEWD.
FAST AS YOU CAN
  ALL.
YOU ANGRY HOUSEWIVES AHHHHH
  LEWD.
BEFORE THIS CROWD TEARS US APART
  ALL.
OH GOD

  LEWD. Weaseal are they here yet? Well go find them look
everywhere. Look in the parking lot.
  ALL.
HEY LEWD FINGERS
WHAT DID THEY SAY LEWD FINGERS
  LEWD.
WELL WE'RE STILL
  ALL.
STALLING FOR TIME
STALLING FOR TIME
STALLING FOR TIME
  LEWD. (*a rap song*)
WE'RE IN TROUBLE HERE
THIS COULD GET ROUGH
IF YOU DON'T GIVE THEM SOMETHING THEY
  COULD GET TOUGH

IT'S THE SORT OF CROWD THAT WOULD TEAR
  YOU APART
AND PUT IT ON VIDEO AS PERFORMANCE ART
SO KEEP YOUR FEET MOVIN, DANCE ANY OLD WAY
CAUSE I'M VERY QUICKLY RUNNIN OUTTA HIP
  THINGS TO SAY
HEY LOOK AT THE WINDOW
HEY LOOK AT THE DOOR
PUT YOUR FEET TOGETHER AND SPIT ON THE FLOOR
I GOTTA A PROBLEM OH OOO WAH EEE
THE HOUSEWIVES AREN'T HERE AND I GOTTA PEE
  ALL.
A-AH-AH

I'M GONNA TAN THEIR HIDES
AND SPANK THEIR PANTS
THROW THEM CLEAR ACROSS THE OCEAN ALL THE
WAY TO FRANCE
SHUT YOUR MOUTH
LISTEN UP YOU DIPS
WE'RE GONNA DO A SING ALONG
SO FLAP YOUR LIPS

(*He is called over by Weasel. The HOUSEWIVES enter.*)

LEWD. Where've you been, man?

CAROL. There was a Volkswagen in the bathroom.

LEWD. Get up there! Get up there! (*in microphone*) And now, folks, the ANGRY HOUSEWIVES!!! (*WENDY shows up at the last minute.*)

WENDI. Wait!!! I'm here!

CAROL, BEV AND JETTA. (*a beat*) Wendi!

WENDI. I'm sorry. (*A pause. They all hug each other.*)

LEWD. (*in microphone*) It's a miracle, folks! The drummer has recovered from her death. Now will the Coyote Uglies please get off the stage and the Angry Housewives hit it???? (*Everyone clears but the HOUSEWIVES. JETTA takes a pose and the band starts.*)

[MUSIC #14: *MAN FROM GLAD*]

ALL.
MAN FROM GLAD, MAN FROM GLAD, MAN FROM

GLAD
MAN FROM GLAD, MAN FROM GLAD, MAN FROM
  GLAD
  JETTA.
I WAS PACKIN' LUNCHES, IT WAS GETTIN' LATE
I WAS REAL TIRED, I WAS STARTIN' TO SAG
WHEN OUT OF NOWHERE I HEARD A MAN SAY
  ALL.
HEY LADY TAKE A LOOK AT THESE BAGS
  JETTA.
IT WAS
  ALL.
THE MAN FROM GLAD
MAN FROM GLAD
GET OUTTA HERE, GET OUTTA HERE
MAN FROM GLAD
  JETTA.
I'VE HAD A BAD DAY
I'VE HAD A BAD DAY
T.V. COMMERCIALS ARE DRIVIN' ME MAD
T.V.
  ALL.
COMMERCIALS ARE DRIVIN' ME MAD!
  JETTA.
WELL HE JUST STOOD THERE IN HIS LITTLE WHITE
  WIG
AND SUDDENLY I STARTED TO SCREAM . . . AH!
THEN ANOTHER VOICE WITH A FAMILIAR RING SAID,
HEY LADY YOU'VE HAD TOO MUCH CAFFEINE
HEY
  ALL.
LADY YOU'VE HAD TOO MUCH CAFFEINE
  JETTA.
IT WAS
  ALL.
ROBERT YOUNG
ROBERT YOUNG
GET OUTTA HERE, GET OUTTA HERE
ROBERT YOUNG
  JETTA.
I'VE HAD A BAD DAY
I'VE HAD A BAD DAY
T.V. COMMERCIALS WILL MAKE ME COME

UNSTRUNG
T.V.
  ALL.
COMMERCIALS WILL MAKE ME UNSTRUNG
  JETTA.
THEN I BACKED UP TO A WALL AND I SAID VERY NICE
DON'T GIVE NO ADVICE TO ME
THEN I RAN INTO THE DEN AND GRABBED A
  BASEBALL BAT
I WENT OVER AND I SMASHED THE T.V.
I WENT
  ALL.
OVER AND I SMASHED THE T.V.
  JETTA.
I SAID
  ALL.
HEY YOU GUYS, HEY YOU GUYS
GET OUTTA HERE, GET OUTTA HERE
HEY YOU GUYS
  JETTA.
I'VE HAD A BAD DAY
I'VE HAD A BAD DAY
T.V. COMMERCIALS, YOW! I'M GETTING PULVERIZED
T.V. COMMERCIALS, YOW! I'M GETTING PULVERIZED
  ALL.
MAN FROM GLAD, MAN FROM GLAD
GET OUTTA HERE, GET OUTTA HERE
GET OUTTA HERE, MAN FROM GLAD
MAN FROM GLAD GET OUT BEFORE I LOOSE MY
  BRAIN
MAN FROM GLAD, MAN FROM GLAD
T.V. COMMERCIALS ARE DRIVING ME INSANE
T.V. COMMERCIALS ARE DRIVING ME INSANE
T.V. COMMERCIAL ARE DRIVING ME INSANE YAH!
AH!!!! (They scream)

(During these choruses, JETTA gets a Man from Glad doll and
variously stomps on it, bites off its head with her teeth and
spits it at BEV, and uses the body to play the cymbal. The
song ends, the HOUSEWIVES take their bows. The men run
towards their women as LEWD quickly kisses CAROL and
grabs the microphone.)

JETTA. Larry, I didn't recognize you! You look so. . . . *pretty!*

LARRY. You know I never do anything half way.

WALLACE. Did you wear the fin?

WENDI. Sure did!!! (*LEWD is handed a ballot by a techy, with a shirt that has weasel written on it in felt tip.*)

LEWD. Listen up, listen up! The judges have made their decision. (*Everyone leans in listening with crossed fingers.*) And the winner is (*By the look on his face we can tell they have lost.*) Big Dick and his Privates!!!! (*He's clearly disappointed.*) Good goin, Guys. Pick up your money after the show. Remember the elimination Slam Dance next week — thanks for comin. (*He shuts off microphone and turns to the HOUSEWIVES et al.*) Sorry everyone. I'm gonna go talk to these judges. (*He exits.*)

JETTA. Shoot. (*Larry hugs her.*) All my life, I've been a wall flower, a Walter Mitty, A hot house plant, A sissy pants — and now I have the chance to get really really strong and it's all over.

CAROL. We gave it our best shot.

LEWD. (*reentering*) Hey, hey — what are these long faces? It ain't over yet.

CAROL. No?

LEWD. No, Simon Membrane of Chain Saw records, loved you guys and said if you got a few more tunes that he'd put it on vinal for you.

LARRY. What good would that do? (*patronizingly*) We only use vinal on our lawn furniture.

LEWD. NO! He wants to make a record, stupid.

LARRY. A record? Oh, well — I'll go deal with that.

LEWD. You can't talk to him dressed like that.

LARRY. Why not, it's a Dior! (*JETTA hugs him, everyone cheers and the finale begins.*)

[MUSIC #15: *FINALE*]

LEWD.
I WAS RUNNIN A CLUB
    TIM.
I WAS RUNNIN A SCAM
    LARRY.
I RAN BACK TO MY MOM
    WALLACE.
I WENT BACK ON MY PLANS
    MEN.
WHEN OUT OF NOWHERE SHE SAID

HEY HONEY I'M PLAYING IN A ROCK AND ROLL BAND
PLAYING IN A ROCK AND ROLL BAND

ANGRY HOUSEWIVES, ANGRY HOUSEWIVES
WORKIN IN A BAND CALLED THE
ANGRY HOUSEWIVES
SINGIN AND-A-PLAYIN
AND IT'S PAYING
AND WE'RE NEVER GONNA BE THE SAME
NO WE'RE NEVER GONNA BE THE SAME
   CAROL.
I WAS SAD AND LONELY
   JETTA.
MY LIFE WAS A JOKE
   WENDY.
I WAS RUNNIN AWAY
   BEV.
I WAS TOTALLY BROKE
   WOMEN.
BUT LOOK AT US NOW SAY HEY HEY HONEY
WE'RE WORKIN IN A ROCK AND ROLL BAND HA
WORKIN IN A ROCK AND ROLL BAND HA
   ALL.
ANGRY HOUSEWIVES, ANGRY HOUSEWIVES
SINGIN AND-A-PLAYIN
AND IT'S PAYIN

AND WE'RE NEVER GONNA BE THE SAME

ANGRY HOUSEWIVES

NO WE'RE NEVER GONNA BE THE SAME
NO WE'RE NEVER GONNA BE THE SAME
NEVER BE THE SAME

(*Blackout*)

[MUSIC #16, 17 *CURTAIN CALL; Exit music*]

PROPERTY PLOT

ACT ONE PROPS

PROP	DESCRIPTION
Electric guitar & amp	Tim
Pink notebook	Bev, must have pages & pictures
Make-up trays	W/creams, tissues
Telephone	
Sandwiches on plate	on a tray made from spaghetti
Tape machine	Bev
Song sheets	
Lewd Fingers flyer	Tim
Five dollar bill	Bev
Briefcase	Larry
Tape machine	Wendi
Punk magazine	Entitled "Bleeding Ear"
Lewd Fingers flyer	Wendi
Wallet	Wallace, with fold out photos
Bottle of pills	Jetta
Phone	Larry
Phone	Tim
Accoustic guitar	Bev
Accordian	Jetta
Handheld cassio	Carol
Bass drum	Wendi
Beer cans	(4) Must be generic
Fish on plaque	Wallace, fins are missing
Drumsticks	Wendi
2 Plates	Bev, of macaroni
Package of hotdogs	Bev, unopened
3 Flashlights	Jetta, Carol, Larry
Jar of grapejuice	Larry
Pen/clipboard	Lewd
5 Dollars	Carol
Champagne bottle	Jetta
Microphone	Lewis/Jetta
Drumset	Wendi
Cassio	Carol
Electric guitar	Bev

ACT TWO

Champagne bottle	}	Jetta
Teddy bear	}	Tim
Overnight bag		
Bag of french fries		
Thick contract		
Towel		
Boxers		Lewd/Carol
Robe	}	Tim
Socks		Jetta/Larry
Shower cap		
Curler		
Magazine		Wallace, entitled "Bleeding Ear"
Fish fin necklace		Wallace
Baby bottle		Larry
Apron, tie		Larry
Plate of Hors D'ouerves		
Champagne		
Glasses		
Man from Glad Doll		Jetta
Ballot in envelope		Lewd

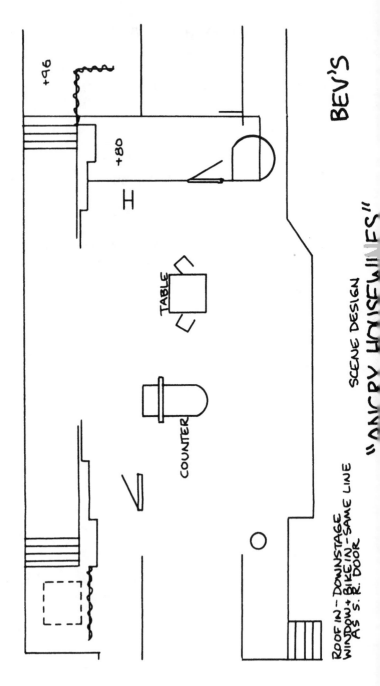

+96

+80

H

TABLE

COUNTER

BEV'S

SCENE DESIGN

"ANGRY HOUSEWIVES"

ROOF IN – DOWNSTAGE
WINDOW + BIKE IN – SAME LINE
AS S. R. DOOR

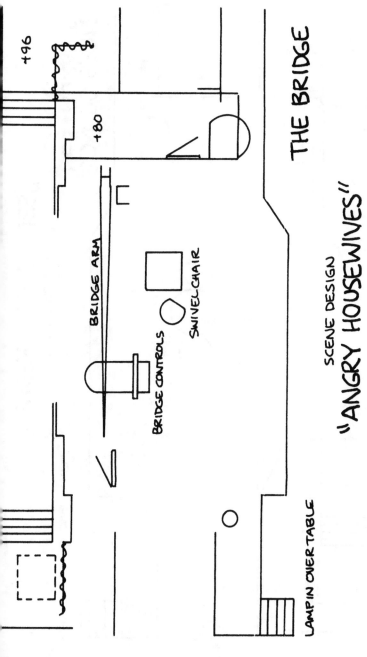

+96

+80

BRIDGE ARM

BRIDGE CONTROLS

SWIVEL CHAIR

LAMP IN OVER TABLE

SCENE DESIGN

"ANGRY HOUSEWIVES"

THE BRIDGE

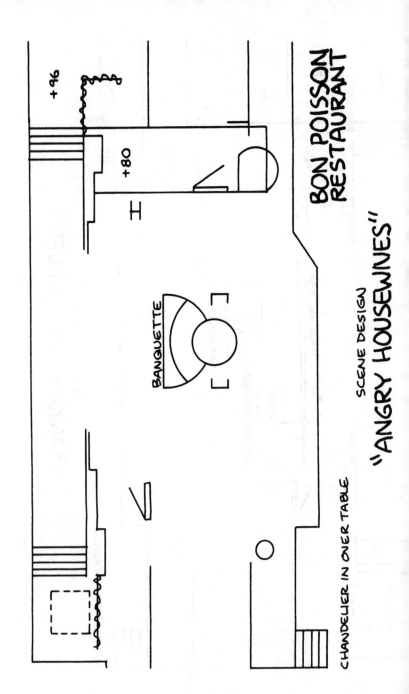

BON POISSON
RESTAURANT

SCENE DESIGN

"ANGRY HOUSEWIVES"

CHANDELIER IN OVER TABLE

+96

+80

BANQUETTE

A.M. COLLINS (*Playwright*) Writer Woman Bird. Artistic Director/Co-Founder of Pioneer Square Theatre in Seattle. Other works include *The Sacred Water Amulet of Lourdes* with Chad Henry and *Emeral Street*, a blues/gospel musical. She now resides in Venice, California, where she is learning to parachute.

CHAD HENRY (*Composer*) is a native Seattleite born earlier this century. He has worked a range of theatre jobs spanning ballet, musical comedy and opera, with personalities as diverse as Bette Midler, Ann Reinking, Pamela Reed, Anna Moffo, Carole Shelley, Tom Poston and the divine Mark Morris, and slaved under award-winning directors Paul Giovanni, John Hirsch, and Dan Sullivan.

SKIN DEEP
Jon Lonoff

Comedy / 2m, 2f / Interior Unit Set

In *Skin Deep*, a large, lovable, lonely-heart, named Maureen Mulligan, gives romance one last shot on a blind-date with sweet awkward Joseph Spinelli; she's learned to pepper her speech with jokes to hide insecurities about her weight and appearance, while he's almost dangerously forthright, saying everything that comes to his mind. They both know they're perfect for each other, and in time they come to admit it.

They were set up on the date by Maureen's sister Sheila and her husband Squire, who are having problems of their own: Sheila undergoes a non-stop series of cosmetic surgeries to hang onto the attractive and much-desired Squire, who may or may not have long ago held designs on Maureen, who introduced him to Sheila. With Maureen particularly vulnerable to both hurting and being hurt, the time is ripe for all these unspoken issues to bubble to the surface.

"Warm-hearted comedy … the laughter was literally show-stopping. A winning play, with enough good-humored laughs and sentiment to keep you smiling from beginning to end."
- TalkinBroadway.com

"It's a little Paddy Chayefsky, a lot Neil Simon and a quick-witted, intelligent voyage into the not-so-tranquil seas of middle-aged love and dating. The dialogue is crackling and hilarious; the plot simple but well-turned; the characters endearing and quirky; and lurking beneath the merriment is so much heartache that you'll stand up and cheer when the unlikely couple makes it to the inevitable final clinch."
- NYTheatreWorld.Com

COCKEYED
William Missouri Downs

Comedy / 3m, 1f / Unit Set

Phil, an average nice guy, is madly in love with the beautiful Sophia. The only problem is that she's unaware of his existence. He tries to introduce himself but she looks right through him. When Phil discovers Sophia has a glass eye, he thinks that might be the problem, but soon realizes that she really can't see him. Perhaps he is caught in a philosophical hyperspace or dualistic reality or perhaps beautiful women are just unaware of nice guys. Armed only with a B.A. in philosophy, Phil sets out to prove his existence and win Sophia's heart. This fast moving farce is the winner of the HotCity Theatre's GreenHouse New Play Festival. The St. Louis Post-Dispatch called Cockeyed a clever romantic comedy, Talkin' Broadway called it "hilarious," while Playback Magazine said that it was "fresh and invigorating."

Winner!
of the HotCity Theatre GreenHouse New Play Festival

"Rocking with laughter...hilarious...polished and engaging work draws heavily on the age-old conventions of farce: improbable situations, exaggerated characters, amazing coincidences, absurd misunderstandings, people hiding in closets and barely missing each other as they run in and out of doors...full of comic momentum as Cockeyed hurtles toward its conclusion."
- Talkin' Broadway

TREASURE ISLAND
Ken Ludwig

All Groups / Adventure / 10m, 1f (doubling) / Areas

Based on the masterful adventure novel by Robert Louis Stevenson, *Treasure Island* is a stunning yarn of piracy on the tropical seas. It begins at an inn on the Devon coast of England in 1775 and quickly becomes an unforgettable tale of treachery and mayhem featuring a host of legendary swashbucklers including the dangerous Billy Bones (played unforgettably in the movies by Lionel Barrymore), the sinister two-timing Israel Hands, the brassy woman pirate Anne Bonney, and the hideous form of evil incarnate, Blind Pew. At the center of it all are Jim Hawkins, a 14-year-old boy who longs for adventure, and the infamous Long John Silver, who is a complex study of good and evil, perhaps the most famous hero-villain of all time. Silver is an unscrupulous buccaneer-rogue whose greedy quest for gold, coupled with his affection for Jim, cannot help but win the heart of every soul who has ever longed for romance, treasure and adventure.

THE OFFICE PLAYS
Two full length plays by Adam Bock

THE RECEPTIONIST
Comedy / 2m, 2f / Interior

At the start of a typical day in the Northeast Office, Beverly deals effortlessly with ringing phones and her colleague's romantic troubles. But the appearance of a charming rep from the Central Office disrupts the friendly routine. And as the true nature of the company's business becomes apparent, The Receptionist raises disquieting, provocative questions about the consequences of complicity with evil.

"...Mr. Bock's poisoned Post-it note of a play."
- New York Times

"Bock's intense initial focus on the routine goes to the heart of
The Receptionist's pointed, painfully timely allegory... elliptical,
provocative play..."
- Time Out New York

THE THUGS
Comedy / 2m, 6f / Interior

The Obie Award winning dark comedy about work, thunder and the mysterious things that are happening on the 9th floor of a big law firm. When a group of temps try to discover the secrets that lurk in the hidden crevices of their workplace, they realize they would rather believe in gossip and rumors than face dangerous realities.

"Bock starts you off giggling, but leaves you with a chill."
- Time Out New York

"... a delightfully paranoid little nightmare that is both more
chillingly realistic and pointedly absurd than anything
John Grisham ever dreamed up."
- New York Times

SAMUELFRENCH.COM

CPSIA information can be obtained
at www.ICGtesting.com
Printed in the USA
BVHW040210160122
626351BV00010BA/304